Other Romance Books By

Breathe You In
Rule Breaker
HOT ICE series
THE CHALLENGE series
The Mobster's Girl
Scored
Thief
Her Dominant Billionaire
Stockholm Surrender
Chains of Command
Accelerated Passion

COLD NIGHTS, HOT BODIES
By Lily Harlem

Chapter One

His strong, masculine arms embraced her nakedness as he forged in farther and deeper. Each powerful thrust of his hips created a starburst of sensations that lapped at her most intimate flesh and floated her higher.

"Oh, Tobias, oh, yes, yes, Tobias," she cried as he upped the tempo to match the racing of her heart. "Please, don't stop, not now it's so..." Saffron squeezed her eyes shut and became lost in the spectacular firework display behind her lids.

Tobias groaned long and hard in her ear. His hot breath ruffled through her hair. Suddenly she was there. It was as if time stood still, everything else ceased to exist. There was just her and Tobias, lying on the soft chaise on his yacht deck with the moon dancing above them. Then, in a glorious release, her whole body went into a series of powerful spasms, clutching him, pulsating around him. It was like nothing she had ever felt before.

He sought her mouth and plundered his tongue in as he curled his hips under and pumped out his own pleasure to mix with hers.

Saffron clung to her new husband with all four of her limbs, her ankles locked over his buttocks and her arms clutching his smooth shoulder blades. A single tear squeezed from her eye.

Tobias lifted his head. "Are you crying?" he asked in a soft, breathless voice.

"No, it's just—"

"You are. Did I hurt you? Oh, Saffron, I'm so sorry. I tried to be careful, keep it under control, but you are just so perfect, so utterly divine it drives me wild."

Saffron put her finger to his lips and pressed. "Shh, my darling, you didn't hurt me, well not after the first bit." She paused to smile shyly. "It was just so special, so loving and so..." She couldn't find the words to describe the consummation of their marriage.

"Amazing." He grinned.

"Yes."

"Good, it's supposed to be amazing your first time." He kissed her tear away.

"Does that mean it won't be the second time?" Saffron whispered as her heart swelled with love for the man she'd just given her virginity to.

"Oh yes, it will be amazing the second time," Tobias murmured, shifting his hips.

Saffron gasped as she felt him hardening again. A fresh wave of desire washed through her.

"In fact," Tobias whispered, "it will probably be more so when I get you to turn around and bend—"

"Ashley, Ashley, for goodness sake get going, will you?"

I lifted my concentration from *The Millionaire's Virgin Bride*, hastily minimizing my screen and turning to Dawn, who stood by my desk with her hands on her hips, frowning.

"Yep, just on my way now," I said, squirming on my seat. The story had me buzzing all over. My knickers were damp and my heart pounding. Tobias was just so perfect—handsome and manly but also sensitive and caring. As he'd cupped Saffron's breasts and stroked over her nipples that first time, I could almost feel the calluses on his palms scratching over my own slight breasts.

"Are you reading that fluffy romantic stuff again?" Dawn asked, flicking her long blonde hair over her shoulders and reaching for her cerise leather handbag.

I'd been rumbled. No point denying it. "Yeah, it's a new release from my favorite author," I said, trying desperately to act as though I wasn't turned-on by a fictitious character taking his wife's virginity.

Dawn rolled her cherry-glossed lips in on themselves. "You need to get yourself some real-life action," she said, her blue eyes sparkling. "Instead of always reading about someone else's fun."

I resisted a sigh. It was all very well for someone who looked like a glamour model to say that. With her silky hair and tanned skin, hour-glass figure and great sense of style, Dawn could have any guy she wanted, and frequently did. Finding romance and all the yumminess that went with it wasn't a problem for her.

Okay, so I *should* be more confident. I *should* wear more "hip" clothes and get myself out there looking for a man. And I knew I should follow her well-meant suggestions about makeup and chat-up lines, but it was just so difficult to leave my mousy comfort zone. I liked it here, it felt safe in my little hole, and my stories distracted me from the man drought in my life. "I know," I said, hoping we weren't going to have the same conversation we'd had a million times already. "I really should."

Dawn opened her mouth to speak but no words came out. Instead she tugged at her bottom lip with her teeth, studied me for a moment then turned and walked away.

"Dawn," I called when she reached the door. "Have a great Christmas."

She smiled over her shoulder as if she knew something I didn't. "You too, Ashley, but right now you have to get going. You'll be late. And don't forget your bag." She pointed at my navy holdall lying beneath the coat hook. "I'll see you in the New Year."

My stomach lurched as I glanced at the clock. Damn, it was gone five. It was always the way once I got involved in a Margaret Rider book. Time stood still for me but kept ticking for everyone else.

I pushed back my chair. Zipped my laptop into its case and dragged on my thick winter coat. It would take three hours to get to The Fenchurch Hotel in Lower Creaton, maybe longer if the traffic was bad—which it was bound to be heading toward the Cotswolds on a Friday only a week before Christmas.

I *had* to go to The Fenchurch. I didn't want to, but I had no choice. My workmates thought I was lucky, a night in a posh hotel and a slap-up meal all at the company's expense. But for me it was torture and it was the second year running I'd been the most productive non-sales employee. In other words, I'd handled the fitting of the most security systems, and so this was the second year running I'd won the Christmas treat.

Quickly I scooted past empty desks—some lay tidy and ordered, others littered with paperwork and potted plants. My overnight holdall was heavy as was my laptop case, and I struggled with the elevator buttons. I made it down to the foyer, said good night to Samantha the receptionist, and stepped out into the office parking lot. Cool wetness brushed my cheeks. Floating down from the dark sky were hundreds of sparkling white snowflakes.

Great, now it would take me even longer to get to the Cotswolds.

Climbing into my faithful neon-blue Volkswagen Beetle, I whacked up the heating and navigated through the London traffic. After an hour I hit the M4, turned on the radio and was soon singing along to Wham's *Last Christmas*. As snow danced in the red taillights of the car in front of me, I dreamed of a log cabin and a handsome man— Tobias would do me just fine. I could get snowed in with him quite happily.

I imagined a roaring log fire at my side and a thick fur rug beneath my naked back, pictured his rugged, unshaven face hovering over me as he promised to take it slow my first time. His dazzling blue eyes would be glazed with lust as he pushed into me, stretching me with his thick manhood, taking me to a place of ecstasy I'd never been to before.

The song ended and I shivered out a breath even though the car was quite hot. My nipples had tightened beneath my sweater and a pulse beat a steady rhythm in my pelvis. Just thinking about Tobias had me aroused. It felt sweet, it felt nice. I took a slug from my water bottle. If these feelings were good in my imagination, what would it be like for real? I was twenty-three and I knew one day I'd find out what sex was like. Sooner or later I'd come out of my shell and grab myself a hunky hero to shag senseless. Dawn always talked about me finding love and romance. It wasn't that I didn't want love and romance, I did, but I also just wanted to do the deed. Get down and dirty, naked and sweaty with someone who knew what he was doing and would get it just right.

Trouble was, guys rarely glanced my way. Who could blame them? I had fine light-brown hair, usually pulled back into a low ponytail. I had no skill when it came to applying makeup, so I didn't bother, and my figure was on the skinny side. There was a definite lack of curves that didn't appear even with baggy clothes. Plus, if a guy in the office or out on the street did look my way it was always a geek I wouldn't even take off my raincoat for let alone my knickers.

No, I was waiting for Tobias the passionate millionaire, or sexy Sebastian from *Ride into the Sunset*, or even bad boy Captain Hawkeye from *Swashbuckling on the High Seas*. They were real men. Men for whom satisfying the women in their lives was all that mattered, after, of course, they'd ensured their millions were well invested, the bad guys caught, and the pirate ship packed full of loot.

A stern voice on the radio warned delays. I sighed, but no sooner had I resigned myself to walking into dinner late than the slip road for my turning appeared. Luck was on my side. I clicked my indicator and whizzed off the motorway. If I remembered correctly it was only a couple of miles to The Fenchurch from here.

The hotel lobby was warm and welcoming after my scramble across the snow-carpeted parking lot. The low lighting glowed and heat from a roaring fire wrapped like a blanket around my cold shoulders. I pulled in the scent of pine from the enormous fir tree decorated with large gold baubles and glanced at the ceramic angel perched on the very top.

After checking in at the high, mahogany reception desk, I took the elevator to my top-floor room.

Pushing open the door, I gasped and my heart did a flip of excitement. Wow. This was so much better than last year's room. This was a suite—a huge, luxurious, decadently furnished suite.

I stepped in and let the heavy door swing shut. A long, burgundy sofa dotted with plump cushions sat before a wall-hung TV and an artificial fire flickered gently from a marble hearth beneath it. A shiny, round table held a vase of enormous ruby roses nestled amongst lush green fronds. Within the rose petals, clear crystals sparkled like ice chips. I dropped my holdall and laptop bag on the sofa and bent to inhale their scent—powder and earth, sweetness and fern.

Still in awe, I wandered through a door to my left and widened my eyes farther. An enormous four-poster bed stood before me covered in a red-and-green checked eiderdown. Matching voile curtains draped from each of its posts. It looked like something from my favorite Regency historical, *The Insatiable Duke of Harrington*.

I kicked off my sneakers and flopped on the bed, spreading my arms and making a snow angel on the covers. "Yippee," I said, looking up at the sagging tartan canopy.

It crossed my mind there must have been a mistake. This wasn't my room. Should I go down to reception and check?

Standing, I studied myself in a large mirror and pulled my hair from its band so it hung in a slight wave around my black roll-neck sweater. No. Why should I? This sort of wondrous mistake never happened to me. And it was about time it did. I would stay here and if someone came and told me to move to another room I would. But unless that happened I'd enjoy my one night of sumptuous luxury. In fact, I'd read the bedroom scenes again from *The Insatiable Duke of Harrington* once I'd got dinner out of the way. I'd pour myself a nightcap and pull up that particular ebook for a good steamy session of literature. Maybe even indulge in a few chapters of *His Maid's Desires* too, if I could stay awake long enough.

Squaring my shoulders and happy with my decision, I glanced at the clock. I had twenty minutes to get out of my "dress-down Friday" jeans and into my smart evening outfit.

I dashed into the bathroom, paused briefly to admire the opulent gold taps and the double shower cubicle, then jacked on the faucet. Tearing the complimentary shower-cap from its cardboard box, I rammed my hair into it and jumped into the steaming water. The hotel shower gel was spicy and rich and the white suds moisturized my skin as they slid down my breasts and legs. I didn't linger, I didn't have time, so I stepped out, reached for a fluffy towel and began scrubbing my teeth with the conveniently provided toothbrush and paste.

Dinner shouldn't take longer than a couple of hours, then I could slip away early. As long as Derek, my regional manager at Safe as Houses, saw me at the beginning of the evening, he wouldn't notice if I wasn't there at the end. No one would notice. No one ever did.

Naked, I walked across the bedroom and into the living room to retrieve my smart black pants and my plain white blouse from my holdall. Opening the bag, I dipped my hand in. Felt soft material and tugged. But instead of black or white emerging from the zipper it was a bright red piece of clothing.

"What the...?"

I didn't own anything that color. I tugged a little more, then held the offending garment out at arm's length. It was a dress, a short flame-red dress with thin shoulder straps and a label on the back that read *Jigsaw*. It wasn't mine. How had it got into my bag?

I stared at it as though it might tell me the answer. It didn't, so I tossed it onto the sofa. I didn't have time for mysteries. Instead, I delved back in to find my pants and blouse. My hand hit a hard shoe. I'd packed patent black Courts with half-inch heels. But the shoe that appeared wasn't a Court, nor did it have a half-inch heel, nor was it black. The shoe in my hand was the same startling red as the dress and the thin, shiny silver heel was at least two inches. I turned it over. Where had it come from? It looked like the shoe from my favorite story of the year before, *Stolen and Seduced*.

Retrieving its twin from the bag, I set the unfamiliar shoes down on the floor. I'd never worn anything like that and couldn't imagine I ever would. *My* shoes must be buried at the bottom somewhere. Clicking my tongue in irritation, I slid my hands around, over the base and into the sides, but there were no more shoes in the bag. Instead, I pulled out a thin cardboard envelope, the clear window displaying a crisscross of black netting. "Fishnet hold-up stockings—pull resistant and guaranteed not to slide" the label boasted.

A flush of heat washed over me.

Fishnet stockings!

This wasn't my bag.

I glanced at the holdall as though it was an alien entity. But it had the same frayed handle as mine and the same ink stain near the base.

It *was* mine.

I turned the stocking pack over. On the base of the pack was a handwritten note in a neat, boxy scrawl I recognized.

My dearest Ashley,

Please forgive me but I've done this for your own good. It's time to come out of your hole and let the world see you for the beautiful and amazing woman you are. Please, I beg you, wear this dress, the shoes and the stockings to dinner tonight—they are all your size. You will look stunning. You will wow the entire company, the best of whom are gathered at The Fenchurch. No one will ever overlook you again.

Please, for me, even if for one night only—shine, my dear friend, shine.

Love, because that is the ultimate goal, Dawn x x

PS—There's makeup in the side pocket, the perfect shade of lippy for you, trust me. Some volume spray for your hair and don't worry, your dull pants and plain Jane shirt will be quite safe with me for the night!!

A burning flame of anger rose in my chest and tears bit my eyes. How could she? And she called herself a friend. No bloody wonder she'd looked so shifty when she was saying goodbye to me at the office. "Don't forget your bag," she'd said sweetly. My mind dragged back over the day. There were several times she could have made the switch in my holdall. I'd gone for a late lunch and she'd been alone in our office for an hour, and also first thing that morning, I'd gone to a meeting in Derek's top-floor office.

As the air enveloped my cooling, naked body, I dropped my head in my hands. What the hell was I going to do? I couldn't wear "that" dress. I wasn't like *her,* all curves in the right places and confidence oozing from every pore. Why couldn't she, if she had to pull this crazy stunt, just have placed a different top in the bag, maybe even red, because it was a nice Christmassy color. I could have worn that with my pants and shoes. Surely that would have sufficed as "coming out of my hole", as she so eloquently put it.

Shivering, I glanced at my jeans discarded on the floor near the bedroom door. There was no way I could wear them. Not for an elegant meal. I scrabbled in the bag for my underwear. "Please let it be here," I muttered.

But oh no. Dawn had switched my trusty full knickers for a lace thong and a matching black strapless bra.

I could have kicked myself for telling her my bra size when she'd asked me a couple of weeks ago. Oh, she was good all right, good at being a sneaky, conniving witch. "Hey, Ashley, they've got a sale on at Selfridges, all small sizes, what do you normally buy?" she'd asked as though butter wouldn't melt in her mouth.

I'd answered as I dragged myself from a deliciously naughty description of Lord Belton savoring his two favorite stable girls.

Well, I just wouldn't go to dinner. I'd wrap myself up in the hotel robe and lounge on the bed with my ebooks.

I stalked to the bathroom and reached for the robe with FH embroidered on the left breast. I would have time to finish *The Millionaire's Virgin Bride* then read all the others I'd planned. It would be fine. In fact it would suit me very well. I slammed my hands into the robe and let the softness embrace me.

The phone trilled to life on the bedside table. I picked it up.

"Ashley, Ashley, is that you?"

"Hi, Derek."

"Ah, good, excellent, you made it through the snow then, it's getting pretty heavy out there and you left later than me. You still looked up to your head in work when I passed by your office."

"Oh, er, yes, just reading through positions." Not alarm positions though, the sexual positions Tobias was dreaming up for his new wife's first night of pleasure. He'd come up with a very naughty idea of bending her over the ship's bridge. A plan of tying her hands to the rail and finding her elusive hot spot from behind. My stomach had flipped as he'd mulled over his plan and I was still waiting to find out if he carried it through. Would it hurt? Would she like it? Would it be the best position to find her G-spot? I'd heard all about G-spots but had no experience of finding my own.

Derek was talking again.

"Um, sorry, what?" I asked, rubbing my temples.

"I'll collect you from your room if you'd like. Save you walking in alone."

"Oh, er." Bless him, he was old enough to be my grandfather and to be honest he sometimes treated me as if I *was* his granddaughter.

"What room are you in?"

I responded, "217," automatically, then kicked myself for my hasty answer.

"Okay, I'll be there in ten minutes. Be ready, poppet."

"But, but I don't think I will be—" The line rang dead in my ear, a sharp monotone hum. "Going for dinner," I said quietly. Damn. I should never have picked up the phone. I should have let him think I was stuck in the snow or maybe even told him I was sick. Or I should have screamed that stupid Dawn had switched my outfit in her pathetic attempt at livening up my life.

I stalked to the minibar. Pulled out a tiny bottle of white wine and poured it into a tumbler. Glugging back the oaky liquid, I thought of the heroines in my books. What would confident-but-waif-like Saffron do in my position? Or the wild and untamed Henrietta from the

Swashbuckling series? I pictured them in a luxury hotel, a sexy outfit and a room full of people downstairs. Would they stay in? Would they curl up with a book? Realization dawned on me as I polished off the wine. Of course they wouldn't stay in. My heroines wouldn't even consider it.

But I wasn't those girls.

I glanced at the clock. I had ten minutes.

Okay, so I wasn't Saffron or Henrietta but I would try on the dress. Just quickly. If it was awful I would actually make myself sick so Derek wouldn't force me to go to the meal. And if the dress was okay, then perhaps I'd think about wearing it, although, who was I kidding, it wasn't likely to be okay, not with my slim hips and lack of chest. On me it would look like a shapeless sack.

I slammed my glass on the table and walked into the living room, letting the robe slide from my arms and land in a heap on the floor. I stared at the black lace underwear. May as well try it on too, I didn't fancy wearing the graying sports bra I'd had on all day, and definitely not the knickers I'd dampened thinking about Tobias.

Oh, the new thong fit like a dream. I'd always thought lace would be itchy but no, so soft, so smooth. And it sat neatly, and surprisingly comfortably, in between my butt cheeks.

The strapless bra held my modest breasts upward, as if they were being displayed on a shelf. The flesh spilled to the very edge of the cups and looked soft and slightly wobbly. Like Dawn's did in the summer, when she wore low tops and laughed. I'd never seen my breasts look so feminine and stared at them in the long wall mirror, fascinated.

But I didn't have the luxury of time so I reached for the dress and slipped it over my head. The material was an indulgence, not silky or satiny but smooth, dense and somehow light too, and it smelled new, like shops and fresh air. As my head popped through the neck and the thin straps settled in the groove of my shoulders, the rest of the dress fell around my body. After fastening the concealed side zip, I looked down, shocked for a moment to see such a bright color on my usually drab torso. The neckline sat the merest fraction above the bra, which meant the soft wobbliness of my new curves was still displayed. The waist nipped in and as I smoothed my hands into the dip between ribs and hips, I realized it hugged my shape perfectly. The flare over my thighs was slightly looser as I walked to the mirror, which meant I could move comfortably, in fact no, more than comfortably, I could walk with the luscious material sliding around the top of my legs—it felt wonderful.

I dragged in a breath and blew it out slowly. Roamed my gaze from my knees to my shoulders. I had never, in all my life, seen my body look so shapely or so curvy. The dress gave me breasts, a waist and hips like Marilyn Monroe. And the color. It made the skin on my arms and chest glow, as though I'd been in the sunshine for a week. Not only that, it reflected onto my cheeks, often too pale this time of year; I looked as if I'd had an invigorating walk in frosty woods.

Turning, I examined my butt. The dress hugged the outline but not so much that it looked tarty. The round globes of my cheeks could be made out but not in explicit detail and there was no hint of the underwear beneath.

I remembered the tale of *A Mistress for Midnight* and how Georgina had worn a red dress to hunt down her man. The red dress had given her the self-assurance and the confidence she needed to pull off her dangerous plan. Red had suited her. Red, it seemed, suited me too.

I glanced at the hold-up stockings. I would need something on my legs *if* I wore this dress to dinner. But seriously, fishnets? Couldn't Dawn have just gotten me a nice, thick pair of opaque tights? They would have suited me much better and been so much more practical. Sliding the stockings from their pack, I tickled my fingertips over the delicate holes. They were so dainty yet so sexy. I couldn't imagine wearing them.

Sitting on the sofa, I carefully maneuvered my toes into the ends of the stockings. Unfurled them and watched, fascinated, as my ankles, calves, then knees and thighs transformed into someone else's. Someone sensual and sexy, someone who had the right shape legs to wear fishnet stockings. I smoothed the dainty lace rim at my upper thighs, stood and let my dress drop over them. My gaze once more went to the mirror. They looked right with the dress. More than right, they looked great. My legs had taken on a different shape, my calves looked a little rounder and more elegant and the tiny diamond holes on the stockings were more subtle than I thought they would be.

Mmm, two out of three couldn't stop me going to dinner. There was no denying the dress *did* suit me and the stockings felt amazing.

I looked at the red shoes sitting on the floor by the sofa. They were bad shoes, sinful shoes, shoes that made you think of stripping naked or pressing the spiked heel onto the chest of a tied-up, aroused man and making him beg for his sexual release. *Stolen and Seduced* sprang to my mind once more. Oh, I loved that book—the thought of being held captive and handing over all responsibility for my pleasure to someone edgy and dangerous was such a naughty turn-on.

But the shoes were where Dawn had gone too far. They would never work for me.

Slipping my toes into the pliable leather, I was instantly two inches taller. I looked in the mirror and was surprised to see myself more than just stretched. The small of my back had arched inward, which jutted out my breasts slightly. My legs appeared longer, my ankles more elegant. Somehow I was balanced.

I took a tentative step forward and felt the spikes dip into the lush cream carpet. But it was okay, the shoes didn't nip or rub and were quite secure to walk in. Lifting my right leg, I studied the silver heel. Pointy and glistening, it was a statement stiletto. A stiletto that said, "I can handle what comes my way so don't start something you can't finish." Daisy had said that to Gray in *The Barmaid's Brew*.

I gulped as I realized that these shoes made me like Daisy. These shoes said I could handle what came my way. I pushed my hands through my hair. But could I? I wasn't a busty barmaid with a gutter mouth. I was Ashley Jones, employee of the year at Safe as Houses Chelsea branch and lover of romance books. I couldn't take what Daisy had taken from Gray. What that guy had done with a whip and a neck-scarf had had me trembling as I'd scrolled down the pages.

There was a sudden sharp bang on the door.

"One minute," I called. "I'll be there in one minute, Derek."

"No rush," he called back, his voice muffled through the wood.

I stared into my green eyes. The hazel flecks at their base seemed even more pronounced. Must be the wine. Was I really going to do this? Was I really going to wear the dress Dawn had sneakily put in my bag? Could I? My figure looked great, there was no denying it, and the shoes and stockings made me feel sexy and hovering on the edge of confident. The underwear beneath the dress a secret only I knew, a sensual and elegant extension of me.

I swallowed a nervous lump the size of a Christmas tree. I *would* do this. And if it went horribly wrong I'd blame Dawn.

"Ashley, how are you doing?" Derek called through the door. "Don't want to miss the pre-dinner champers now, do we?"

"Just coming," I said, grabbing the volume hairspray Dawn had provided. I didn't read the label, just finger brushed my waves then, flicking my hair around as though I were on some cheesy advert, liberally sprayed the lemon-scented mist. It worked. I suddenly looked as though I had twice my normal amount of hair. Who would have thought that was possible in five seconds?

Knock, knock.

"Coming," I called, reaching the makeup bag from the side of the holdall and tottering up close to the mirror. I added a quick flick of powder, a sweep of jet-black *Double-Ur-Lash* mascara and finally a slick of fire-engine red lipstick—phew! It was so red!

"Coming now, Derek," I said, shoving the lipstick into my small, black clutch bag and giving my wrists a squirt of my floral perfume, which thankfully Dawn hadn't removed. I dashed to the door, rubbing my wrists together, and yanked it open.

Derek stood before me, a navy pinstripe suit straining over his generous belly and a green tie dotted with tiny Christmas crackers hanging beneath his double chin.

"Wow," he said, his eyes widening behind his glasses. "Is that you, Ashley?"

A knot of doubt clenched my stomach. What the hell was I doing? I was stupid to think I could pull off a look like Dawn's. I would be a laughingstock.

I stepped backward into the room. "I, er don't feel so good," I said, my mouth forming a lie about nausea and sickness, a contagious rash and a sky-high fever.

"Well, you certainly look good," he said, following me in. "In fact, you look, if you don't mind me saying, absolutely stunning."

I turned to him, a bubble of hope rising in my chest. "Do you really think so?"

"Hell, yeah." His gaze flicked to my toes then back to my face. He blew out a breath that made his jowls wobble. "Blimey, if I was thirty years younger and didn't have my Janice, you would be in trouble, young lady." He gave a good-humored chuckle. "I love your party look, glad you don't wear it to the office though, the guys on the next floor wouldn't get anything done, particularly Gareth."

I smoothed my hands over my hips and looked at my shoes.

"Really," he said, his voice quieter, "you look perfect for the Christmas party except..."

I gulped. "Except."

"I'm a guy and I don't really know about this sort of stuff, but do you have a pair of earrings or a necklace? My Janice always puts something a little sparkly on, especially for a Christmas night out, she says it makes her feel nice." He smiled gently at me.

"Oh, yes, actually I do have a necklace...somewhere." I dug into the side pocket of the bag and pulled out the silver necklace my parents had bought for my twenty-first birthday. It was a thin link chain with a tiny diamond-encrusted heart pendant.

"Here, let me," Derek said, reaching for it with his podgy fingers.

I turned and scooped up my puff of hair to expose the back of my neck. He lifted the necklace and fastened the clasp at my nape.

"Thanks," I said, studying my reflection in the mirror one last time. I looked good, Derek was right, what I was wearing was perfect for a Christmas party and, it seemed, was perfect for me too. I tried to feel angry at Dawn, but staring at my new image all I could feel was gratitude. I should have listened to her earlier, years earlier. Because now I felt like Saffron and Daisy and Henrietta all rolled together.

I licked my bright-red lips and tasted a hint of the strawberry gloss the lipstick was infused with. I was ready to come out of my hole.

Chapter Two

Derek and I walked into Morgan's Champagne Lounge only a few minutes late. The place was buzzing as people stood chatting, laughing and drinking at the wide wooden bar. Waiters in black tuxedos and neat bowties moved around carrying silver trays heavy with canapés and flutes of champagne.

I stepped in and stood a fraction behind Derek's wide body. A gut-twisting nervousness wound through me and I suppressed a sudden wave of nausea. What if my dress was hugely inappropriate after all? What if people laughed at little Ashley Jones trying to look sexy and feminine? Perhaps the stockings and shoes were going too far, maybe they made me look like the office tart instead of the office mouse. I knew which I preferred.

Derek turned to me and smiled. He handed me a flute of sparkling bubbles that misted over the top of the glass and dampened my hand. "Cheers," he said, clinking rims. "Here's to another successful year at Safe as Houses."

"Yes, cheers." Urging my hand not to shake, I took a sip and glanced around. There were more men than women in the room. But the half dozen or so women, mostly older than myself, all wore dresses of varying clinginess and party colors. I noticed Rachel from the Huddersfield branch, ten years my senior, looking elegant in a figure-hugging purple number and her hair piled on her head in a chignon. Her shoulders were set down and her head tipped as she spoke with a smile.

Watching her, my own shoulders relaxed. As I set them down I felt the arch pull in the small of my back again. It felt nice, as if I was proud of my body. Hell, I was. I'd just looked in the mirror. With my new curves I was a similar shape to Rachel. Why shouldn't I stand tall and proud? The nausea and nerves subsided and I took another sip of champagne, holding out my little finger like I'd seen ladies do in the movies.

"I'm so glad the merger with Camilla Homes has happened this year," Derek said. "It's incredibly beneficial for the company. I'm pleased to have seen it happen before I go."

"Go?" I asked, snapping my attention away from Rachel and the arch in my back. "What do you mean go?"

"Ashley, poppet. I'm sixty-four, sixty-five on New Year's Day. I've decided to retire. Janice and I have always dreamed of a cruise and the appeal of days out on the golf course has been growing for some time now."

"But, but there is so much more I thought you wanted to do at Safe as Houses."

"Well, there is more I want to do, you're right. But not at Safe as Houses. Out in the big, wide world. Retirement is an adventure, not just for me but for Janice too. She's been planning a whole host of things to keep us young and occupied over the next twenty years."

I looked at his eyes, sparkling with enthusiasm. "Well, in that case I'm very happy for you. But of course I'll miss you terribly. You've been a great boss."

"And you've been a great employee. You've always got your head in the computer working hard. But I'm sure I'll be in to say hi to everyone from time to time." He took a mouthful of his drink. "But I don't want a big fuss, a party or anything, so Ray Burgess is going to announce my retirement at the end of tonight and then I'll hand over quietly to my successor during the holidays."

I couldn't imagine going into work and not seeing Derek there. Not having him lead meetings in his firm but gentle manner. Who else would make the effort to bring in cakes and fizz when it was someone's birthday? Who else would be so understanding about the need for an occasional "duvet day" when the weather was horrid and Monday morning just too much to handle?

"Derek, Derek, how are you? So glad you made it through the blasted weather."

Ray Burgess, owner of Safe as Houses, stepped up and pressed his hand onto Derek's shoulder.

"Hi, Ray," Derek said, smiling.

"And who is this?" Ray turned to me. He was the same age as Derek, with thinning hair scraped back over his balding crown. He too, was pot-bellied and his tie had pictures of tiny houses on it. On the roof of each house a mini LED flashed like one of our little alarm boxes.

"You must remember Ashley Jones," Derek said. "She joined us here last year."

Ray's gaze slid down my body, over my chest, my hips and to my shoes. "No, I can't recall that we had the pleasure of being introduced," he said, returning his gaze to my face just before I was weirded out by his gawp.

"Pleased to meet you, Mr. Burgess." I remembered us being introduced the year before. But what was the point in arguing? I clearly hadn't been memorable.

He smiled and shook my hand, wrapped it entirely in his hot, slightly damp one.

"Ladies and gentlemen," a loud voice boomed from the doorway right behind us. "Would you all please take your seats for dinner?"

Gratefully I extracted my fingers from Ray's and turned. The head waiter was gesturing toward the restaurant opposite the bar.

"Come on," Derek said to me. "Let's go find some seats."

"I want you to sit at my table," Ray said to Derek. "I need to pick your brains about a few things before you-know-what." He winked exaggeratedly.

Derek nodded. "Sure thing," he said, stepping away from me with an apologetic smile.

The ripple of nerves in my chest turned into a wave of panic. If Derek was sitting next to Ray then who would I sit next to? I moved with the crowd into the restaurant and glanced at Rachel—she was nice, perhaps I could sit with her. But she was laughing and linking arms with Jeremy, the team leader from Cheltenham branch. My eyes searched the room for someone else familiar. Chairs were being scraped on the floor and the hum of conversation increased as people settled themselves at the dozen or so large, round tables.

I gulped back the last of my champagne. No one else seemed to have a moment's hesitation about where to sit. For them it was like putting on a pair of slippers or making a cup of tea. Effortless.

For me the urge to run, to turn and flee, was like a primitive instinct. Why the hell was I here? I should just go to my room, read about Tobias' kinky wedding night. Find out what it would be like to be tied to the bridge of a yacht and have a sexy millionaire squeeze orgasm after orgasm from me.

I fiddled with the heart pendant resting just below the hollow of my neck. Run or stay? Run or stay? There were hardly any unclaimed seats left. My gaze scanned the room, flicking over the large plumes of Christmas flowers standing centrally on each table and the tinsel strung around the picture rails.

Suddenly I spotted a free seat at Rachel's table, two places away from her. I remembered all my heroines. None of them would turn and run from a room of people when there *was* a free seat.

Bracing myself, I tilted my chin and stepped toward the table, praying that no one would beat me to it. My hips rolled as I walked and the warmth of the room settled on the exposed upper mounds of my breasts. As I approached the table, the person who would be sitting between Rachel and me turned and looked straight at me.

My heart stuttered. It was Shane Galloway. The *delectable* Shane Galloway who'd won the overall most productive salesman of the year three years in a row. I'd admired him from afar last year and watched him dance after the meal with Ray's wife Rose. I gulped. I was offering myself up for a mealtime conversation with a guy so out of my league he might as well live on Mars.

Shane was gorgeous in a rock-star, devil-may-care kind of way. He had jet-black hair that just touched the top of his white collar, the skin on his face was pale and his eyebrows dark and heavy. There was a sprinkle of stubble on his chin and above his top lip. Already he'd loosened his navy-blue tie and undone the first button of his shirt.

I kept putting one foot in front of the other. Felt and saw his gaze slide down my body. His attention hovered for a moment on my rolling hips before rising to my face once more. Then he was standing, standing and reaching for the chair I'd planned on claiming.

Oh god. It was already taken?

He'd intended on sitting next to someone else? He didn't want me to sit there. He was going to move it. I was going to have to turn away.

I hesitated. Looked into his dark eyes and held my breath.

"Here," he said in a smooth voice, tilting the left side of his mouth into a smile. "Allow me."

If I'd thought the rush of nerves earlier was intense then this was like a tsunami. Shane Galloway actually wanted to sit next to me? Wow, the power of a red dress, fishnet stockings and killer heels.

I stretched my glossy lips into a matching smile and prayed I didn't look as shaky as I felt. "Thanks," I said, stepping up to the table.

He touched the chair against the back of my knees. I sat, knotted my fingers in my lap and crossed my ankles.

"Hi, Ashley," Rachel said, leaning forward as Shane sat his tall frame back down. "You look...er...really well." Her blue eyes were wide behind her spectacles as she absorbed my new look. "Have you been on holiday or something?"

"Er, no, no holiday."

Everyone at the table turned to me. Even a young, pimpled guy opposite was peering around the tall floral centerpiece to stare.

"How are you, Rachel?" I asked, trying to keep my voice casual.

"Fabulous, thanks and this is great, isn't it? They always do such a lovely job at The Fenchurch."

I nodded and reached for the slim glass of water a waiter set before me.

"Have you two met before?" Rachel asked, flicking her gaze between Shane and me.

"No," Shane answered, smiling my way. "I don't believe I've had the pleasure." His lips looked soft and sensual, his top left tooth crooked by a millimeter over the right one and his eyes sparkled as though full of sin. Dark, naughty, expert sin. The sort of sin bad-boy pirates and dukes intent on satisfaction had in their eyes.

"Ashley," I said, unknotting my fingers and holding out my hand. "Ashley Jones. I'm from the Chelsea branch."

He took my hand. Curled big, warm fingers around mine and squeezed gently. "Shane Galloway, Huddersfield branch. It's lovely to meet you, Ashley."

A snake of sensation washed up my arm, ran across my shoulder and settled in my chest. I pulled in a breath and was treated to a lungful of his light aftershave. He tipped his head slightly as he carried on staring into my eyes. He pulled in a deep breath too.

"I, er, it's a pleasure to meet you as well." I extracted my hand and dragged my gaze from his. If I wasn't careful I could almost fool myself into thinking he was attracted to me. I wasn't an expert in this sort of thing but in my books, lingering handshakes, prolonged eye contact and inhaling perfume were all connected to human attraction.

"So, congratulations," he said, reaching for a seeded bread roll.

"For what?" I asked, watching him tear the roll in half. His fingernails were neat and perfectly square. He had a faint line on his left ring finger.

"For being employee of the year at your branch," he said, smearing a thick wedge of butter onto his roll.

"Oh, yes, that. And you too." I reached for my own roll although I suddenly didn't feel hungry. There was a heaviness in the pit of my stomach like hunger but I didn't think food would sate it. A quiet read of *Pounding Without Sound* would fill the gap. Marie and Travis getting it on together in the restroom of a Boeing 747 was always a good read when I needed something I couldn't quite put my finger on. Or rather, I needed to put my finger on.

"Yeah," he said. "Personally I didn't sell quite as much as last year because I've been a bit distracted." He bit into his roll.

"Oh," I said. "Why is that?"

He swallowed. "It's been a crap year." He leaned back and his soft suit jacket touched my bare shoulder. "What with one thing and another."

"Like what?" I didn't move away from the warm, slightly scratchy touch of his suit. It felt nice, it felt up close and personal.

He turned to me and lowered his voice. "I got divorced in March and took an unpaid month off to visit a mate in Australia, and then in September, I started a part- time university course in marketing, which has taken me out of the office one day a week." He smiled. "Still, hopefully the course will make me even more productive in the future. It's already given me some great ideas."

"Well, you've still been top seller in Huddersfield despite taking time off and being on a four-day week."

A waiter set bowls of steaming creamy soup in front of us.

"Yes, I came joint with Rachel, that's why we're both here."

I glanced at Rachel chatting animatedly to Jeremy.

"And I'm sorry about the divorce," I said. "It must have been tough."

"Yeah." He shrugged. "We'd only been married eighteen months. But it seemed she preferred my best friend to me so what could I do?" He bent his head over his bowl and scooped up a spoonful of soup.

I watched the way he blew gently on the liquid before opening his mouth. A small dent appeared in his cheek, then his Adam's apple bobbed low as he swallowed. How could anyone choose someone else over him? Not only was he drop-dead gorgeous, he was charming, successful and right up there with Tobias and Bret and all the others in my books. Plus, I'd bet my right arm he'd know just what to do in the bedroom. I'd bet those square fingers knew which buttons to press and that mouth knew just how and where to kiss. His ex-wife was a fool. But her loss was my gain, because here I was, little mousy Ashley, sitting next to hunky, newly single Shane Galloway.

He glanced at me. "I know what you're thinking," he said.

I bet you don't.

"What?" I asked, taking a sip of my own rich soup and thoroughly enjoying a tingle of desire for a real man instead of a fictitious one for a change.

"How could I not have seen it coming?" he said.

"Did you?"

"No, not at all. Although looking back the signs were there. Hell, they both disappeared for twenty-five minutes at our wedding reception."

I gave a sympathetic frown. "Do you think they were…at it?"

"I don't think, I know. She threw the information at me in an argument last Christmas. They'd been shagging in the ladies' toilet for heaven's sake." His brown eyes captured mine and he sighed. "I'm sorry, Ashley. I don't normally meet someone and start boring them with this."

I shrugged. "It's good to talk about bad stuff that's happened. It gets it off your chest."

"Yeah, but it's history, I guess with the New Year coming up it makes you think of all that's happened, but now I'm looking forward to starting afresh."

"Is that what you're going to do?"

"I've already done it. Since I got home from Oz I've been getting my teeth back into life." He smiled broadly. "I know I've got a good career if I just keep working hard and I wish Mandy and Jared well. No hard feelings, no bitterness, because that would just drag me down."

"Very sensible, and of course you wouldn't want to be dragged down any longer." I drew my gaze from his face, took another sip of my soup, and let the creamy potato coat my tongue and warm my throat. I forced myself not to think of all the dragging down I'd like him to do to me. Had we been on *The Lost Soul*, he a pirate and me a willing wench, he could have dragged down my garter and petticoats, my pantaloons and corset all day, every day until we reached shore.

"And what about you, Ashley?" His gaze settled on my mouth. I licked my lips and hoped I didn't have a sprig of stray herb stuck in my gloss. "What are you hoping for next year?" He glanced at my hands, the way I had his. Was he checking for a wedding ring? Surely not.

"Mmm, I don't know really." I could hardly tell him that losing my virginity was top of my to-do list. That finding a hot hunk to screw me silly was becoming increasingly pressing.

"Are you going for any promotions at Safe as Houses?"

"No, I'm happy with what I'm doing. I like chatting to customers and not having to take any of the work home with me at night. When I go out the office door, my time and my mind are my own."

"Very sensible," he said, taking a sip of the wine the waiters had just served. As he set the glass down his gaze strayed a little farther from my mouth, floated over my neck and into the hollow of my throat. "I like your necklace."

"Thanks." Instinctively I pressed my finger to it. "It was a present."

"From your boyfriend?"

"No, no boyfriend. My parents gave me it as a birthday present a few years back."

"It's very pretty," he said, still looking at it. "Just like you."

My chest tightened. My breath hitched and a wave of intense heat spread up to my cheekbones. He'd just called me pretty. No guy had ever said that to me before. I placed my spoon down and it clattered against my bowl.

"I'm sorry," he said, leaning back as a waiter gathered plates. "Not very smooth of me, I know." He shrugged. "I'm kinda out of the game at the moment, guess I've lost my touch and subtlety never was my strong point."

I opened my mouth to speak but no words came out.

"Have you finished, miss?" a waiter asked over my right shoulder.

I nodded vigorously.

The waiter cleared away and Shane reached and grabbed a Christmas cracker. "Here. Pull this with me."

His action sparked the rest of the table reaching for their crackers and I was glad of the deflected attention from my blush. Bangs, cries of surprise and hoots from wheezers rang out. I clutched the crinkled end of the gold cracker Shane offered and braced.

We both pulled and it split in two with a loud crack. My chest wobbled as I laughed. It surprised me, I laughed harder and my chest wobbled some more. Shane chuckled and for the briefest of seconds his glance hit my quivering breasts.

"Excellent," he said, scooping up our loot from the starched-white tablecloth. "A tiny torch for when the lights go out later." He flicked it to life and flashed the weak beam onto the palm of his broad hand.

"And the joke?" I said, reaching for the curl of white paper, "is..." I paused. It wasn't a joke at all. It was a proverb.

"What is it?" Shane asked, leaning in close again.

"The things that are really for thee, gravitate to thee," I said over the squeals and cracks coming from other tables.

"Very appropriate," he said with a smile, and taking it.

"What do you mean?"

He folded it in half and poked it into his inside breast pocket. "I think I've come up with enough cheesy lines for the first course, don't you?"

The main meal was traditional turkey with all the trimmings followed by Christmas pudding and brandy sauce. Shane and I chatted about our Safe as Houses colleagues and compared offices, commutes and parking complaints, then the conversation moved on to movies. I read more than I watched but still offered up a couple of the year's big releases to discuss. It seemed Shane was a keen cinemagoer and preferred the big screen to sitting at home. "Better appreciation of the cinematography," he said seriously.

I told him about the holiday I'd taken to Egypt in the summer with my parents—the mighty pyramids and the flies that had eaten me alive. He kept the whole table entertained with a story about a snake in his boot in the outback, and how he and his friend had tempted it out with raw sausage and captured it in a net.

I watched him talking and thought how perfectly masculine the texture of his skin looked—just the right amount of stubble over an angled jawline. I rubbed my fingertips together in my lap and wondered what his cheek would feel like to touch. What it would be like pressed against mine. He turned to me and smiled as he stretched his arms wide to show the length of the snake. I imagined his sharply stubbled chin on my chest, on my stomach, on the inside of my thighs. I squeezed my legs together as a tiny tremor buzzed in my pelvis. In *The Barmaid's Brew*, Gray had tormented Daisy with the roughness of his cheek on her inner thigh, touching and scratching until she'd begged for more, demanded that he go higher and take her intimate flesh into his mouth.

A sudden loud clinking snapped my attention away from the erotic image and I turned to see Ray standing two tables away, banging his spoon against his glass.

"Ladies and gentlemen," he boomed. The room fell silent. "Thank you all so much for coming tonight despite the atrocious weather conditions, it really is very much appreciated."

"All this for free, no chance I was missing it," a heckler behind me shouted.

A rumble of laughter and *hear, hear* echoed around as Ray held up his glass. "I can assure you it's not free for me." He laughed. "But I'm not complaining, you guys have once again exceeded all my expectations with the way you throw your efforts and your skills into making Safe as Houses the biggest, most reliable, most recommended security company in the country."

A cheer rang out and several people hooted on paper trumpets. I looked back at Shane. I couldn't help it. He was like a magnet, and an image of us in the same position as Daisy and Gray had suddenly appeared in my mind's eye.

"And," Ray said, "before the disco begins next door and we dance off those calories, I would just like you all to raise a glass to my very dear friend and colleague, Derek Finlay, who is retiring in the New Year." He turned to Derek who was sitting beside him. "You will be sadly missed but I know you have a very busy and very exciting retirement planned and I wish you all the best."

Derek smiled, though I had an inkling it was slightly strained. He wasn't big on being the center of attention.

"Thanks," Derek said, color rising on his cheeks. "It's been a pleasure to be part of such an inspiring company."

"To Derek," Ray said, lifting his wine high before taking a sip.

"To Derek," the room said as one.

"To Derek," I added quietly, feeling a weight tug at my heart. Out of all the people at The Fenchurch, it was me who'd miss Derek the most. He was part of my daily life and I couldn't imagine who'd ever be able to fill his shoes.

"May the party begin," Ray shouted. He clapped his hands and pointed through a darkened archway.

Thumping music suddenly belted out from the room next door. The tinsel- decorated arch came alive with flashing neon lights and the restaurant erupted in a burst of energy. "Dance until you can dance no more—it's Christmas!" Ray bellowed around cupped hands.

My feet absorbed the pounding beat, which vibrated right up through my body.

"Excuse me," Shane said, standing.

I watched as he turned and walked away. His broad shoulders shifted beneath his suit jacket with each of his long, ground-eating strides. A sagging hole gaped in my stomach. He'd gone. Clearly he'd been up for the meal and that was him done for the evening. Either that or he had his eye on someone else he wanted to be with.

He slipped from the room and I turned back to the table, heart heavy. Everyone was pushing back their chairs, finishing dregs of wine and hot-heeling it to the dance floor.

"Come on, Jeremy," Rachel said, grabbing his arm and smiling broadly. "Show me your moves."

Jeremy laughed. "You reckon you can handle it?"

"Oh yeah, bring it on, big boy." She giggled, half walking, half skipping toward the archway.

Jeremy dashed off behind her with a broad grin on his face.

The pimply young guy sitting behind the flowers stuck his head around them and looked at me. He gave a shy smile. "Wanna dance?" I could hardly hear him over the music but I lip-read the words.

I didn't really want to dance with him. But he had a flicker of hope in his eye and his smile was slightly shaky. I didn't have the heart to say no.

"Sure." I pushed up from the table. "Just one dance and then I'm going to turn in. It's been a long day." Not to mention my heroes and heroines were calling me.

He grinned and stood. He really was very tall, and very slight. His suit hung on him as if he were a wire coat hanger and his neck looked overly long and very pale.

We walked through the arch and my eardrums were blasted with Manic Machines' risqué Christmas hit, *SlipKnot*. The dance floor was heaving with gyrating, thrusting bodies. Arms waved and bodies twisted amongst the bright flashing lights.

We began to bop on the outskirts of the group. He smiled again, exposing his yellowing teeth, and jigged from one foot to the other. He stepped closer, or rather lunged, and I hopped back. I didn't want any body contact. This was a mercy dance and the sooner it was over the better. I was already thinking of Tobias and Saffron and curling up under the duvet on my four-poster bed. I was going to have such literary fun.

I glanced at Jeremy and Rachel. She'd locked her hands behind his neck and he was swinging her around. They were having a wild time. They were both single and it was clear they were going to end up enjoying hot, naked, sweaty activities together. Making their own heat to combat the icy chill outside, doing the sort of stuff my characters got up to and what I longed to do.

A flicker of jealousy lit within me, but it quickly turned to alarm as the music switched to a slow ballad. Pimply guy reached for me. An excuse to escape grew in my mind.

I stepped backward and bumped into an immovable body.

"Excuse me," a deep voice rumbled over my shoulder. "This young lady owes me a dance."

I turned and looked up into Derek's smiling face. His cheeks were flushed and the disco lights reflected in his thick glasses.

"Derek," I gasped, full of relief. "Sorry," I said to my skinny suitor. "He *is* my boss." I pulled a semi-apologetic expression and turned away. I didn't really feel bad. He wasn't my type. There would be someone out there for him but it definitely wasn't me.

Derek put a chaste arm on my waist and wrapped my small hand in his big, soft one. I smiled up at him. "Thanks," I said.

"You looked like you needed rescuing. I've seen that look before."

"You have?"

"Yes, when that supply postal guy asked you out in the spring." He laughed. "To his mother's poetry recital."

I groaned at the memory. I hadn't known whether to be monumentally insulted or flattered. I think I'd settled on insulted. "Yeah, no wonder he was single if that was his best date offer."

"Yeah, must have been hard taking a knock back in front of the whole office though," Derek said with another huff of amusement.

"He shouldn't have asked me out in front of everyone."

Derek's face turned serious. "But what about now, poppet? Is anyone taking you on dates to the West End or for long, lazy walks around Hyde Park on a Sunday morning? Gareth, maybe?"

"Oh no, there's nothing between me and Gareth, we're just friends. But I'm a romantic at heart and I live in hope of finding *the one*." Why people thought Gareth and I might hook up was a mystery. He was a mate, that was all. There was no spark between us.

"Love and romance will definitely find you," Derek said firmly. "Probably when you least expect it. Look at me and Janice. There I was, standing in the queue at Covent Garden buying candy floss for my little sister and suddenly there she was, smiling at me from behind a pink, sugary cloud, all shy and pretty with big blue eyes."

I smiled. I'd heard the story before. It was his "love at first sight" speech.

"We stepped out together the next night and were married six months later," he went on. "I don't believe in hanging around. If there is something you want, go for it. Some things in life are worth taking on the 'terrier' attitude for even if it's not really in your nature. Don't you think?"

I nodded. He was right. Maybe I should take on the terrier attitude. There were things I wanted, no make that needed, and I wasn't any closer to getting them at the moment.

"You just have to grab hold of opportunities," he was saying. "Grab hold and don't let go, it's the only way sometimes."

That was all very well, but I needed an opportunity to get rid of my damn virginity. To someone handsome and dashing, someone sophisticated and experienced, and that opportunity just didn't seem to be coming my way. But maybe with this new look, this new flicker of confidence Dawn had shown me I possessed, I had more chance of achieving my aim in the New Year. I wasn't so naïve to think that just the look would change me. I needed to change inside too. I needed to be more proactive in looking for opportunities and if I found them, like Derek said, I had to go for it.

The song ended and in its place another slow ballad started.

"Perfect," Derek said, grinning down at me. "*Lady in Red* couldn't be better since I'm dancing with the only lady wearing red in the room." His face got serious and I noticed a few beads of sweat on his forehead. "Seriously, Ashley, I'm really going to miss the office. Janice is so excited and so am I, but it's going to be hard not seeing my team every day and sharing a laugh over our morning coffee..." His voice trailed off and he looked over my left shoulder. His arm tightened on my waist and he spun me around.

My feet stumbled as I came face to chest with Shane Galloway.

I looked up.

He stared down.

He'd ditched his jacket and tie and his white shirt shone neon in the disco lights. Where he'd undone his collar a small collection of dark hairs curled on his chest.

"May I?" Shane asked Derek, though his dark gaze stayed captured with mine.

"Be my guest," Derek said, releasing me and stepping backward. "To tell you the truth, I could do with wetting my whistle." He made a drinking motion with his hand. "I'll catch you later, Ashley. Don't forget what we were talking about." He gave me a quick wink then was swallowed by the crowd.

I stood, arms at my sides, as a rush of joy washed through me. Shane was still at the party and not only that, he was looking at me with the same dark twinkle in his eye he'd had earlier.

"Come here, lady in red," he said, reaching for me with both hands. I stifled a gasp as he confidently wrapped one arm around my waist and caught my hand in his. He pulled our knotted fingers against his chest and tugged me close.

My breasts pressed against our joined hands, the exposed flesh peeping over my dress just touching the back of his knuckles and the fold of my own thumb. He swept his tongue over his bottom lip, coated it in a damp sheen, and kept his hand exactly where it was.

Reaching up, I rested my palm over his shoulder and felt the hardness of taut muscle beneath his shirt, lean and strong, firm and toned. He set up a gentle sway to the music and I followed his lead, absorbing his body heat. "I thought you'd gone," I said.

"I had to make a call. My sister was driving back from Scotland after visiting a friend. I wanted to make sure she'd made it okay through the snow."

"And did she?"

"Yeah, she's home safe and sound." His mouth broke into a smile and small creases darted toward his temples. "Sipping cocoa with the cat curled up on her lap."

"Good, I'm glad," I said, mesmerized by his handsome face.

He slid his hand up my back and ducked his head to my ear. I breathed in deep as the skin on his jawline came close to my face. He smelled divine, a "fresh from the shower scent" that reminded me of open water and clean air.

"Just as well," he murmured. "I've just looked outside. We're well and truly snowed in here, not much I could have done to help her if she'd got stuck somewhere."

"We are?" I asked. "Snowed in?"

"Oh, yes. We're trapped, no one is going anywhere, in or out of this place."

As he spoke, his hot breath washed over my neck and generated a tickle over my scalp. I'd never experienced a feeling like it before. It was pleasurable. It was exciting. It was sexy as hell. "At least it's nice and warm in the hotel and there's plenty of food and drink," I managed.

He pulled back and grinned. "Yeah, but if this ancient heating system breaks down we may have to get inventive with ways to keep warm."

I looked into his eyes. They held a cheeky glint and one side of his mouth twitched, creating a tiny dimple in his right cheek.

"What do you suggest?" I asked.

"Well." He tipped his head to the side and narrowed his eyes as if contemplating options. "We could always just drag extra blankets on to the beds, make hot water bottles and drink tea or, and this is probably more advisable, we could share body heat, generate our own warmth. I hear it can save your life to get close and cozy with someone on a cold winter's night."

"Close and cozy," I repeated in a whisper, hardly daring to acknowledge in my mind what he was suggesting.

"Mmm." His face was so near to mine, hovering just a hair's breadth away. "Close and cozy and...naked."

My body jerked. It was involuntary. I hadn't meant to jump within his arms. But his words were like whips of sensation that traveled around my brain then sent darts of pleasure and terror to all the corners of my being. Naked. With him? Me with Shane Galloway?

He huffed and pulled his head back. "Sorry," he said. "Guess I'm the only one here hoping the heating breaks down, eh?"

"Er, no, not at all." I averted my gaze from his. My thoughts were spinning. What was I supposed to say to that? If I said I wanted the heating to break down I was saying I wanted to get close and cozy and naked with him—hell, I did. And if I said I didn't want the heating to break down that was saying I wasn't attracted to him—and I was. I was so attracted to him I wanted to stay in his arms all night. I wanted to kiss him, lick him, adore him all over. I wanted to do the things Tobias and Saffron did on their first night together, and then the things Daisy and Gray did and...

Heat rose on my cheeks again. Another blush was about to attack. Burying my head into the crook between his chest and his shoulder, I let my hot skin rest on his soft shirt. He smoothed his hand up my back, settling it beneath my hair and stroking a gentle circle.

"Sorry," he whispered. "I didn't mean to be so full on. It's just been a long time since I held a beautiful woman in my arms. I've been so caught up in work and study and all that."

"It's okay," I murmured, sliding my hands over his shoulders and linking them at the nape of his neck. I tipped my face up to look into his dark eyes. Opportunities, Derek had said. You've got to grab them like a terrier and not let go, even if it's hard to go against your nature, it's what you've got to do. Pulling in a breath, I swallowed a lump of apprehension. "I want the heating to break down too," I said, beating down a wave of anxiety at the meaning behind my words. We were talking in code. Flirting with each other and testing the water. I'd just told Shane Galloway I wanted to get naked with him.

Suddenly the music switched. A hard rock song came on, deafening me with its meaty base. Couples around us snapped apart and began to jig with gusto, waving their arms and kicking out their legs. Shane and I stayed locked together.

"You wanna get out of here?" he asked, his face suddenly serious and his eyebrows pulled low.

I sucked in a breath. The disco air was hot and the plethora of perfumes and sweat mixed with the smells of dinner suddenly too strong. The music was unbearably loud and the floor overcrowded. "Yes," I said, nodding. "Let's get out of here."

Chapter Three

As we walked back through the near-empty dining room, Shane scooped up his jacket and I grabbed my purse. Derek and Ray sat in the corner, deep in conversation and deeper in a bottle of Bordeaux. I was grateful Derek didn't look up as Shane and I slipped out.

"Do you want another drink first?" Shane asked, gesturing at the Champagne Lounge.

I glanced into the bar. It was empty except for staff. Did I want another drink first? First before what? Sex? No, I'd had enough alcohol. If I was going to have sex with Shane then I wanted to be *compos mentis*. I wanted to feel, experience and remember every tiny detail of our time together.

"No, I'm fine, thanks. I might just nip to the ladies' though." I pointed to the restroom opposite.

"Sure." He shrugged and tossed his jacket over his shoulder.

I pushed into the bathroom, but didn't use the toilet, instead going to the counter, leaning over the sink and staring at my own reflection. I hardly recognized myself. The lipstick had stayed in place perfectly and a matching rosy glow had settled on my cheeks. My hair was still bouncy and full around my head and it flowed over my shoulders in a soft river. The diamonds in my necklace glistened from the hollow of my throat and my breasts shifted up and down with each breath.

But my eyes had changed since I'd last looked at them. Not the long black lashes or the color of my irises, but the depth, the base. Staring some more, I tried to work out what was so different. And then it hit me. My eyes were filled with desire, real desire. They were brimming with lust for a man who wanted me. Not a fictitious hero in a book, the figment of someone else's imagination, but a real, live flesh-and-blood man. They sparkled, clear and sure. Shane was exactly what I needed. There was no cause for nerves or hesitation. I'd been waiting my whole adult life for this night and finally it had arrived.

Standing straight, I skimmed my hands into the dip of my waist and over the soft rise of my hips. Red was so good for me, it symbolized my passion about to be unlocked, my female desires and my new "grabbing opportunities" mantra.

I pushed through the restroom door feeling sure of my decision and ready to embrace my night with Shane Galloway's delectable body.

He was leaning against the opposite corridor wall, one leg bent and his jacket hooked onto his finger and hanging down his arm. He looked like a dashing millionaire waiting for the woman of his dreams, confident that his empire was being run smoothly while he saw to other, more carnal needs.

His gaze lifted to my face and he pushed away from the wall. "You okay?" he asked in his soft Northern accent.

Smiling, I dragged in a deep breath. "Yes, fine."

His attention dropped down my body, unashamedly roaming right to my toes then all the way back up again. "Your room or mine?"

I couldn't help the tremor in the center of my belly. His appreciative gaze was like a gentle caress, it was as though he was actually touching me all over.

"Mine," I said quietly then added, "I got lucky and they gave me a suite."

His face cracked into a grin. "Perfect. Absolutely perfect."

We rode the lift in silence. I shifted on my heels and stared at the swirling brass motif above the lift buttons. My knees were a little weak and not quite my own. When the doors slid open, I was grateful for the arm Shane offered.

Stopping at the second room on the left, I slipped my keycard into the lock, pushed the door and walked in.

Shane stepped in right behind me and the door shut. "Wow, this is fabulous," he said, blowing out an admiring breath. "You sure did get lucky with this one." He walked to the sofa and dropped his jacket over the back. "You've got a fire and a huge TV and everything. How cool is that? And I love that picture." He pointed to a large abstract canvas. It looked like a sunset, pyramids and a wonky camel but I couldn't be sure.

As he admired the artwork, I glanced around. A maid had been in, tidied up my strewn-about clothes and wineglass and turned the fire on. The four table lamps cast buttery shadows on the floor and ceiling.

I moved toward the bedroom and peeked in. The thick bedspread had been turned back and there was a single chocolate on the pillow.

After placing my purse next to my laptop case, I turned to Shane.

"Come here," he said, holding out a hand. "It's warm in front of the fire."

I forced my shoulders to relax. I didn't want him to see how nervous I was about being alone in a hotel room with a hot guy.

Stepping toward him, suddenly my shoes didn't feel so comfortable anymore. I paused, wriggled my feet out, first the left then the right, and abandoned them on the deep pile.

"Hey, you're really little," he said with a chuckle.

"You're just tall," I said, drawing up in front of him. The fire was warm, but heat from his body was more potent and more alive than any flame.

He reached out and cupped my cheeks in his palms. "They say opposites attract," he murmured. "And my god I'm so attracted to you, you wouldn't believe."

Utterly mesmerized, I watched as he poked out his tongue and smoothed it over his bottom lip. His nostrils flared as though he was dragging in a deep breath then his lips parted.

I stood, arms hanging at my sides, knees buckled, as he lowered his head and pressed his mouth to mine.

It was a gentle kiss, not wet and not dry, the perfect combination of smoothness and maleness. I parted my mouth and held my breath as he delicately traced my bottom lip with his tongue, then I captured his taste—wine and water, man and musk. Pulling in air, I was treated to his gorgeous light scent again.

"You're so sweet," he murmured, pulling back a fraction. "Like a little sugary doll."

Pushing to my toes, I pressed my lips to his, wanting more of his taste and his desire.

This time the kiss quickly turned hotter and harder. Still he kept my face cradled in his hands, holding me just where he wanted me as he probed his tongue deeper, searching for mine with the hot, insistent tip.

I lifted my tongue from the base of my mouth and tentatively touched it to his. He gave a small groan and slanted his head. Our tongues tangled and I reached up and curled my hands into the material of his shirt. Hung on as our breaths quickened and our mouths fed off each other. I became lost in his kiss, he was all I could think of. His taste, his smell, the way he was holding me was my entire universe. Bubbles of pleasure erupted deep within me. A crazy new need flowed like lava through my veins, settled in my breasts, seeped between my legs and spread over my skin.

He pulled back and dropped his hands from my face.

I opened my eyes.

His mouth was shiny from our kiss and his eyelids heavy. "Lose this," he whispered, sliding his fingers beneath the thin shoulder straps of my dress.

I prayed my heart wouldn't give out, it was beating so hard and fast. He wanted me to take off my dress. Of course he wanted me to take off my dress. We were going to have sex for heaven's sake. The dress *had* to come off.

I slid down the zip and the material loosened around my ribs. He stooped, gripped the hem and began to lift. It smoothed up over my thighs and waist and air breezed over my buttocks, which were exposed by my thong.

He straightened, his expression heavy with concentration as he carried on peeling the dress upward. I stretched my arms above my head and was blinded momentarily as the dress brushed over my face.

Shane didn't drop the dress on the floor. Instead he shook it straight and laid it on the back of the sofa. Instinct made me want to cross my arms over my breasts, flatten a palm over the shockingly tiny piece of lace that made up the front of the thong Dawn had provided. But I forced my arms to remain still, hanging at my sides as he turned to me.

"Phew," he said, blowing out a breath and scanning my legs. "I must have been a really good boy this year to get stockings filled so sweetly."

I couldn't help but notice there was a long, hard bulge straining against his fly. My stomach flipped and I quickly averted my eyes and glanced down at my legs, which were encased in black fishnet. The scalloped tops looked fine and dainty against my pale thighs. The flickering shadows from the fire caressed their outline and even I had to admit, they looked damn good.

"You think so?" I asked nervously, trying not to dwell on the size of the bulge I'd just seen.

"Hell, yeah." He stepped back over. "I must have accidently found a cure for cancer or secured world peace to get such a great present."

A small, apprehensive giggle escaped my lips. "You like the stockings then?"

"I've never liked stockings more than at this moment in time," he whispered onto my mouth. "Promise me you'll keep them on, even when you take everything else off. I want to feel them rubbing against my skin when you're wrapped around me."

I shivered in a breath at the wonderfully erotic image he'd just created. "I promise."

He glanced down at my jutting breasts. "You're beautiful, you know that." He traced his finger over the soft curve at the top of my right breast and into my newly deepened cleavage.

A dart of pleasure shot to my nipples, as though the weight of my breasts had doubled under his touch. They were suddenly tingly and tight.

"You do know that, don't you?" he said again as he traced over my left breast. "Of course you do, I'm sure you've been told by plenty of guys."

"Er, no," I said, pressing my palm over his shirt and feeling his hard pectoral muscle shifting slightly beneath.

"No, you don't know it or no, you haven't been told?"

"I...well...I..."

His gaze captured mine and he tipped his head to the side. "Are you okay?" He stilled his finger.

"Yes, it's just..." I slid my hand up to his shoulder and held on for support. I had to tell him. I didn't think I could go through with "wrapping myself around him" if he thought I was experienced and confident. I'd be sure to disappoint or let him down somehow. He deserved to know. Besides, Saffron had told Tobias, so had Felicity in *Lord Morton's Maid* and Skye had left a note for Ralph in *Optimum Pleasure*. All my heroines told their men it was their first time. It was the right thing to do.

"What is it?" Shane asked again, his eyes searching mine.

"I-I haven't, you know, done it before."

"Done what?" He creased his forehead into a frown.

"You know, it, had sex." I stared down at my dark, stockinged feet. They contrasted sharply with the golden carpet. "I'm a virgin."

His whole body snapped backward. It was as if he'd been electrocuted. "Jesus," he said, shoving his fingers through the hair on the crown of his head and stretching his elbows out to the side. "What the hell?" He stared at me with wide eyes.

I crossed my hands over my chest. "I'm sorry." A shard of fear sliced into my heart. He didn't want me anymore. Now he knew I was a virgin he no longer desired me. He'd wanted an experienced lover for the night, not some naïve little girl.

"And you let it get this far before you told me?"

"What do you mean? We haven't done anything other than kiss."

He huffed. "Yeah, one hot kiss with you looking like the best damn Christmas present of my life." He shoved his hands down his waistband and appeared to re- arrange the bulge behind his fly.

"I'm sorry. Partly for letting it get so far and..." I paused. "And partly because you appear to be in physical discomfort."

"There's no need to be sorry," he said, glancing at the door and pulling his hand from his pants.

"Well, clearly there is." I was getting frustrated now. "If I wasn't a virgin we'd be heading into the bedroom by now. Clearly my inexperience has put you off."

"I had that in mind actually," he said, pointing at the deeply cushioned sofa next to us. "It's wide and soft and by the fire. It would have done just fine."

I tightened my arms around myself. He'd wanted to make love to me on the sofa. Just the thought of it sent a tremble up my spine. It would have been so perfect. So sensual and sweet.

He rubbed his hand around the nape of his neck. His dark, tousled hair fell over his ears and he cast his eyes downward.

"I had to tell you," I whispered, shivering despite the blasting heat of the fire.

"Thank goodness you did. Imagine if I'd just gone for it, not knowing. It would have been catastrophic."

"What do you mean?"

"I haven't been with a woman for a while," he said, frowning. "And you in those damn stockings and with your sexy little body." He pulled in a deep breath. "I was just about to lose control. It wouldn't have been the gentle initiation to sex that you deserve, Ashley, it would have left you dazed and confused and wondering what kind of beast you'd invited to your room."

He didn't look like a beast, and he certainly hadn't touched me like one. His fingertip on my flesh had been gentle and reverent. Although now he mentioned it, when he'd looked at my stockings there'd been a glint in his eye that had made me wonder how much control he had.

"Does it change things between us so much?" I asked quietly.

He sighed. "Of course it does."

"But why?"

"Because your first time should be special, with someone you care deeply about...love."

"I care about you."

"But we've only just met."

"But I still care about you more than any other guy I've ever met." I swept my hands down the exposed skin on my body. "No one else has seen me like this before."

His eyebrows twitched as his gaze roamed my underwear. "Lucky me."

I frowned. "Shane, I want to do this, with you. Tonight."

"But surely you want more than..." He shrugged and clamped his lips into a tight line.

"Than what? Go on, say it. We're both adults. We both know what we're doing."

"Okay, surely you want more than a one-night stand to give away your virginity to?"

My jaw clenched. Of course I knew that's what this was. But having it said aloud hurt. Quickly I shoved that stupid bit of hurt way down deep. I had a more pressing matter to concentrate on and I wasn't about to let this opportunity slip through my fingers. "I'm twenty-three, Shane, I'm still a virgin and I don't want to be." I pulled in a deep, determined breath. "I've chosen you over a bunch of losers who've chatted me up and asked me out over the years. It's taken me a long time to find someone I want to have sex with. One-night stand or not, I want you to make sure I'm not a virgin when I wake up in the morning." I put my hands on my hips and narrowed my eyes. "Do you think you're man enough to do that?"

"Oh, I'm man enough all right. I'm also man enough to walk away and stop you making a mistake you'll never be able to undo."

"But how can it be a mistake if it's what I want?"

"Because you don't know what you want. Why can't you see that?"

"How dare you." I stepped up to him, poked out my index finger and pressed it against his chest. "You have no idea what I want *or* need."

He looked surprised by my sudden rise in voice and stern tone.

"I'm a virgin not an idiot. I know about love and lust and I know there's a difference. I also know I want to be initiated into the world of sex by someone handsome, intelligent, experienced and...and..."

"Expert?" He raised his eyebrows.

I tutted and lowered my finger. "Yes, that will do quite nicely, expert. I want someone who isn't going to fumble and falter. I want someone who knows which buttons to press."

"Buttons?" He gave a hesitant smile and a lock of hair fell over his right eye.

"This is not funny, you know."

"Oh, believe me, there's nothing funny about the ache in my pants I can't do anything about." He pushed his hair from his face.

"Of course you can." I lowered my voice, gentled my tone. "I've been reading up and I know what you need too, I know what you'd like, Shane. It doesn't have to be boring because it's my first time."

"What have you been reading?"

I shrugged. "Stuff."

"Elaborate."

"Stories about sex, men and women, things they do other than just the missionary position."

A flicker of interest crossed his face. "Like what?"

"Things like oral sex," I said quietly. "A woman taking a man into her mouth, sucking and licking until he comes down her throat." I paused, sensing his heightened attention at my words. "I want to try that."

"Anything else you been reading about?" he asked, shifting from one foot to the other.

"Yes, tying up a lover and doing whatever you want to their bodies, making them squirm with pleasure and cry out for more." I could hardly believe I was saying all this stuff.

"You want me to tie you up?" His eyes widened.

"Not my first time." I silently congratulated myself on not blushing.

"Your second?"

"Maybe, perhaps I'll wait 'til third though." I reached for the first, fastened white button on his shirt.

Opportunity. Grab it like a terrier.

"There's something else I want to try before that," I whispered.

"And what's that?" he asked, watching me undo the button. His voice had calmed, his body was still. He was no longer stealing glances at the door.

"I want to try it from behind."

"What, in your—?" His eyes snapped up to mine.

"No, no, just from behind so I can find my G-spot."

"Jesus, you have been reading up."

I undid the next button and the next and reached for the cuffs. "Yes, I like to do my research." I tugged his now-undone shirt from the waistband of his smart black pants. "If I'm going to do something, I like to do it properly."

"Me too," he said in a quiet, calm voice.

Shoving the shirt over his shoulders, I stepped in real close and let my breasts press into the tightly coiled hair sprinkled over his chest. "Which is what makes you so perfect for my needs," I said, sliding the shirt down his arms and letting it fall on the floor.

"Damn, you've nearly got me persuaded," he said, lowering his head. His lips rested against my temple and I heard him swallow tightly.

I pulled back and looked up at his dark eyes, they were thick and velvety. I parted my lips and held them a whisper from his. "Will this persuade you?" I cupped my palm against the taut material of his pants and gave his cock a firm, confident squeeze.

Chapter Four

Shane dragged in a sharp breath. "Bloody hell," he muttered.

"I want you, Shane, I want you to take my virginity."

"Ashley, are you sure?"

"More than sure." Over his pants, I rubbed my palm up the length of his erection, marveling at its solidity and size. "Please don't leave, not now, because that would be the worst thing to have ever happened in my life. That would be something I could never undo." And it was certainly something that didn't happen in my books.

Suddenly his lips hit down on mine, strong and assertive. "If it's really what you want then I'm not going anywhere." He breathed into my mouth. "Except to bed...with you, right now."

"Yes, yes, it's what I want." My stomach flipped with excitement. I'd persuaded him to stay. I'd grabbed my opportunity—quite literally.

I looped my hands around his neck, pressing the entire length of my body into his until his cock was squeezed tight between us. My heart thumped and my skin was alive with new, interesting, wild sensations.

"I told you, it's been a while for me," he said, pulling back to look at my face. "Your vampish little virgin thing may have me reaching the finish line early if you're not careful."

"I'm sure we can make more than one finish line."

He chuckled and I sensed the last shred of tension and uncertainty leave him. "Yeah, you're right." He smoothed his hands to the back of my bra. "We have all night and we're well and truly snowed in so what's the rush?" He undid the clasp with a finely tuned movement and the lacy cups fell from my breasts.

"No rush," I murmured even though impatience was bubbling like a cauldron deep within me.

His gaze drifted downward. "You have great tits," he said. "Pert and pretty." He stroked his thumbs over my nipples. They twisted into tight buds, as if straining for more of his attention. "Has anyone even done this to you before?" he asked.

"No," I said on a shaky breath, watching his every move the way a hawk watches a mouse. "Never."

"So I'm guessing no one has done this either." He bent and kissed over the rise of my right breast, his soft lips inquisitive as he traced the mound.

"No," I managed.

Shifting his shoulders, he pulled my erect nipple deep into his hot mouth.

I buried my hands in his thick mop of hair. "God, no," I gasped. "Not that either."

He switched to the other breast and used his hands to feed my hypersensitive flesh gently into his mouth. I closed my eyes and tipped my head to the ceiling, it felt divine, warm and wet, tingly and strong. His tongue was injecting white-hot lust into my veins.

"Ah, you're sweet all over," he said, straightening and pulling me close again. My damp breasts pressed against his scratchy chest. "I'm going to make this right for you, Ashley. I'm honored you've chosen me. You won't regret it."

"I know." I touched my fingertips to his stubbled jawline. "I know, Shane. I trust you."

With one quick movement he scooped me into his arms. I clasped my hands around his neck as his strength surrounded me. He began to walk toward the bedroom.

"We're not doing it on the sofa?" I asked.

"No, we'll do the sofa later, your first time should definitely be in bed," he said, stepping through the doorway. His eyes widened. "And wow, what a bed."

I glanced at the four-poster. Huge and luxurious, it did look the perfect place to lose my virginity.

Shane carried me over and set me down so I was sitting on the edge with my feet on the floor. I watched in silence as he moved the darkly wrapped chocolate from the pillow and placed it on the bedside table.

Straightening, he looked down at me, his gaze so hot it was like a lick of flame across my bare flesh. He frowned and took a leather wallet from his back pocket, flipping it open and pulling out a green-foil-wrapped condom. "I've only got one," he said, "but when we need more there's a machine in the gents' downstairs."

I nodded, pleased he was thinking about contraception and safety. I couldn't, anticipation of what was going to happen in the next few minutes had taken over my brain. I was buzzing all over. It was as if I was in my own novel, I was the heroine and he the hero. And my goodness, what a perfectly exquisite hero I'd been blessed with.

Shane toed off his shoes and peeled off his socks. Reached for the button on his pants and yanked the zip free. He pushed them down, stepping out and kicking the knot of black material to one side.

I sat motionless, just staring at the big bulge tenting his navy cotton boxers.

"You okay?" he asked, stilling in front of me.

Clearing my throat, I looked up his long, lean body shrouded in shadows from the one low lamp in the room. His abdominal muscles were faintly defined, his pectoral muscles square and his nipples small, dark discs. "Yes, I'm fine."

He stepped closer. His groin came level to my face and the heady scent of his skin radiated toward me.

Desperate to touch him, I traced the line of fine silky hair that led from his navel to the waistband of his boxers.

He tensed.

I glanced up at his face. "Can I?" I asked.

The corner of one side of his mouth twitched. "Be my guest."

Pulling the boxers away from his cock, I exposed the round, smooth head. Tugged lower and released his thick shaft corded with bulging veins.

He reached for the material and with one smooth movement shoved the boxers so they landed at his feet.

I stared at his cock. The head was flushed a deep, berry red and the shaft rose from a nest of jet-black pubic hair. But more than anything else I was mesmerized by the sheer size. Sure, in my books the heroes were always blessed with wide girths and impressive lengths, Captain Hawkeye particularly. But none of my novels had prepared me for coming face-to-face with a real cock. A real, live enormous one.

As if sensing my apprehension, Shane murmured, "It's okay, honey, we'll fit." He reached out and tucked a stray strand of hair behind my ear.

"Are you sure?" I glanced up at his face. From where I sat it seemed like a physical impossibility .

"Of course I'm sure," he said with a smile. "We'll just take it nice and slow. Make sure you're ready."

What could I do but trust him? I looked back at his cock. I wanted to touch it, wanted to learn its shape and texture with my fingertips.

Reaching tentatively forward, I wrapped my hand around his shaft. It bobbed upward and I squeezed, squeezed until I could feel unyielding cords of hardness beneath his taut, soft skin.

He hissed in a breath. "Jesus, your fingers are so tiny on me." He placed his big hand over mine and increased the tension of my grip. I became aware of his pulse beating rapidly through his cock into my palm.

"Should we put the condom on?" I asked, wondering how long it would be until he came.

"No, not yet." He pulled my hand up his shaft then pushed it back down. "I'm in control." He moved my palm again, right from the base in his pubic hair to the rim of his glans. Then repeated the movement a little faster, a little harder, as if showing me how he liked it. It was such an honest, real gesture that it pulled a string in my heart. I wanted him to have pleasure too. This wasn't just about me and my lingering virginity.

Increasing the pace, I felt the velvety hardness grow more steel-like. A small drip of pearly liquid appeared in his slit. With my other hand I reached forward and spread the silky moisture over the smooth surface of the head of his cock. It was hot and glossy, delicate but at the same time tough. I dipped the tip of my index finger under the rim of his glans, headed back up to the slit and swirled and circled over it and into it.

"Oh, fuck," he said, stepping back and forcing me to release him. "I'm not going to stay in control if you keep doing that."

A little pop of satisfaction burst in my stomach that he'd enjoyed my actions.

He stepped out of his boxers and dipped his face to mine. "Time for you to lose *your* underwear," he said in a husky voice. "Pretty as it is, it's gotta go." He slid his fingertips into the dip of my waist and tugged on the impossibly thin lace of my thong. "Lift," he instructed, glancing down my body.

I did as he asked and he rolled the miniscule piece of material over my hips and down my thighs. I sat back on the cool sheets as he looped the thong over my ankles and discarded it next to his clothing.

He dropped to his knees, planted a kiss on my left kneecap and smoothed his hands up the back of my calves. "I have a feeling we're going to be great together," he murmured, kissing the lower part of my thigh through my stockings and creating a tremble that went straight to my clit.

"You have? You do?" I asked, staring at the top of his tousled hair.

"Yeah." He rose and caught my mouth with his. "We're going to have a seriously hot night, one I'll make sure you never forget." His long body pressed me down against the sheets.

"We are? I won't?"

"Oh yeah, and we're definitely not going to have any problems with hypothermia."

My shoulders landed on the bed and my nipples brushed against his hard chest. His erection —long and hard, steely and demanding—touched my hipbone. This was it, he was about to enter me. Anticipation made me giddy. I shut my eyes and hoped my body would do as it was supposed to.

His kisses left my mouth and headed down my neck. Smoothing my hands over his broad back, I absorbed the heat and power radiating off him and wondered again when he was going to get the condom on.

"I just need to know one thing," he murmured.

"Mmm, what?"

He cupped my breast and lapped at my straining nipple.

I arched my spine as desire for more coursed through me.

"Shane," I murmured when he appeared to have forgotten he'd asked me a question. "What do you want to know?"

"Have you come before?"

"What do you mean?"

"You know what I mean?" He looked up at me with dark, sultry eyes. His long lashes cast shadows on his cheeks. "Have you ever brought yourself to orgasm?"

I brushed my fingers through his hair, swept it back from his face and thought about the many times I'd rubbed frantically at my clit while reading or fantasizing about my fictitious heroes.

"Yes," I whispered, not breaking eye contact. "Once or twice."

"Good." He grinned. "Then you know what we're aiming for."

I gave a small nod. Admitting I masturbated was easier than I'd thought it would be. I'd never discussed it with anyone. Ever.

His kisses dropped to my ribs and he began an intense investigation of my right side. "Shane. Please..."

"Patience." He moved his mouth to my stomach. "Be patient, Ashley, and I'll make it so good for you. So, so good." He dropped farther down my body and settled between my legs, pushing at my inner thighs, spreading them wide.

I snatched in a breath and pushed to my elbows. My fishnet stockings pressed against the outer edge of his shoulders as he knelt on the floor. He was kissing over my small patch of dark-blonde pubic hair toward my hipbones and exploring the delicate skin on my inner thighs with his fingertips.

"Shane, I—"

"Shh, lie back."

"But—"

"You said you wanted a lover who knew what he was doing," he said, looking up and catching my eye. "Believe me, I know what I'm doing. Now rest back and enjoy."

"Oh god," I murmured, fisting the sheet and dropping back to the bed. I felt so exposed, so open and vulnerable. Here was a man, Shane Galloway, sitting between my spread legs, winding his fingers up my thighs and tickling his tongue through my pubic hair. I was so visible, every tiny crease and fold of my most private parts exposed. My smell, my taste, it was all laid out for him to sample.

"Relax," he murmured. "I consider this a specialty of mine." He pressed a hot, wet kiss to the top juncture of the lips of my sex.

His mouth, in such an intimate place, was like an electric shock. Every nerve in my body went on red alert. Fight or flight? Could I really let him do this?

Specialty?

Before I could move away, he dipped his tongue downward and searched out my clit. He found it and swirled around the needy nub.

A guttural groan that I had no control over vibrated up through my chest. His tongue felt so good, wickedly good, and stroked a need I had so deep inside it had become part of my soul.

He wasted no time in getting busy and suddenly, instead of feeling vulnerable I felt powerful. This was wonderful, this was sating a desire that had been rumbling, no make that thundering around for far too long.

Shane murmured something approving as his hands forced my legs wider, stretching me open for his inquisitive fingers. He traced over my flesh and touched where his tongue was working. Revealing my clit from its hood and spreading out pliable folds. Fingertips, his tongue, fingertips, his lips, his tongue. It felt divine and I handed myself over to sensation. Pressure began to build within me and I screwed my eyes tight shut only to be greeted with a deep crimson color behind my eyelids.

He carried on licking. Thrashing my clit as his fingers searched out my entrance. Quiet lapping sounds filled the air along with our heavy breathing and my small moans.

"Shane, oh god, it feels so good," I moaned, squirming my hips. "So, so good."

He didn't answer. Instead he pushed a finger into me, just one, just enough for me to clamp my pussy muscles around. But it wasn't just my internal muscles that tightened, it was my whole body. This was the first time anyone's finger other than my own had entered me. It felt sweet, alien, I was swelling around him as blood raced to my pussy from every other part of my body.

He didn't let up with his mouth as I adjusted to his new invasion. Thrashing and sucking, he brought my clit to a state of frenzy. I was building to a climax a million times faster than when I did it myself. The rhythm he'd set up was perfect, more than perfect.

"Shane, oh, yes, just there, I'm going to...I'm going to come."

He entered me with another finger and pushed up, higher, wider. I stretched around him as he pumped in and out, making love to me with his fingers and tongue.

Suddenly I was there. I cried out long and loud as extreme pleasure claimed me. Deep within my core he forced higher. A stitch of erotic pain mixed in with the crescendo of my climax. A climax so hard and fast that I twanged forward and clamped my legs around his shoulders.

"Ah, ah, ah, yes, that's it." I tangled my hands in his hair and pulled his head from between my legs. The release had produced a sensitivity that was unbearable.

His attentions left my clit but he kept his fingers inside me. I pulsed around them. My muscles were not my own. Throbbing and spasming, they clamped over and over as sweat pricked my skin and the sound of my rapid heartbeat raged in my ears.

His face was flushed and his lips shiny with my moisture as he stared at his fingers buried deep within me.

"Blimey," he said. "You're so responsive."

"What kind of woman wouldn't be with you doing that?" I asked on a wheezing breath.

He looked up and grinned—a grin that held more than a little male pride. "I'll take that as a compliment."

I flopped back on the bed. The fact that his fingers were lodged in me had gone from feeling alien to natural all in the space of one orgasm.

"But that was just starters," he said, looming up over me.

"Starters?"

"Yeah, we just had to get that job out of the way."

"What do you mean?"

"Seeing if your hymen needed to be broken."

"And did it?"

"No, I don't think so. Did it hurt when I put my fingers in?" He shifted them slightly and caressed the inside wall of my pussy.

A tremor tapped up my spine. "No, no, I don't think so, maybe a little when I came and you pushed higher."

"I couldn't feel anything blocking the way," he said with a small shake of his head. "There didn't seem to be anything there."

A flood of anger welled within me. "You don't believe me. You don't believe that I'm a virgin." How could he question my honesty? It would have been a damn sight easier not to tell him.

"Hey, hey, yes, I believe you," he said quickly. "I'm just saying it's good, we're good to go. You don't have to have an intact hymen to be a virgin."

I frowned at him but felt my anger subside.

"I was insanely attracted to you when I didn't think you were a virgin, Ashley, and now you've told me you are, I'm excited and flattered about taking it. So believe me, the only thing that is going to happen next," his voice lowered and his eyes glinted, "is I'm going to fuck you."

The way he said "fuck" had me instantly flushing to a fevered state again. Such a naughty word from his shiny mouth still slick with my desire was as erotic as hell. I slid my hands down his chest, searching for his cock. "So just do it," I said, enjoying the new tide of lust and confidence washing through me. I wanted his glorious big cock inside me. Not just his fingers. I wanted to feel it, all of it.

He chuckled and dropped a sweet, musky kiss to my cheek. "Oh, I am going to, don't you worry about that, plus now we know it's not going to hurt you." He maneuvered us so we were laying the right way on the bed with our heads on pillows.

I was still breathing hard, my insides still wet and swollen with desire. I missed his fingers inside me.

"Hang on a second," Shane said, reaching across me for the condom. I watched as he ripped the wrapper with his teeth and pulled out the ring of latex. He flopped back on the pillow, strained his neck forward and placed the almost transparent condom over the head of his cock. "Necessary evil," he muttered, pinching the end with his thumb and finger.

"Have you ever not used one?"

"Yeah, Mandy and I were trying for a baby. Just as well it didn't happen. It would have been an added complication now."

I didn't say anything.

He too was silent for a moment. "It's good without though." He efficiently rolled the condom down his shaft. "You feel more connected, more in touch. It feels a whole lot hotter and a whole lot tighter, like going with a virgin." He threw me a cheeky grin.

"So don't use one," I said, wanting him to have the full experience. "I'm clean."

"Are you nuts?" he asked, finishing his task and moving over me. "Clean is only half the issue. You really want a baby from a one-night stand?"

"I guess not." I wished he wouldn't keep saying "one-night stand" even though it was true.

"Absolutely not," he said firmly.

"Do you still want kids?" I asked.

"Yeah, I'm twenty-nine, it would be nice to think it would happen sooner or later." He slid his body farther over mine, settled between my legs and straightened his arms so he was suspended high above me. "No more baby talk," he said, looking down at our bodies. "I want you to watch as I enter you."

I followed his line of sight. His big cock was jutting toward my spread pussy. The air between us smelled of sex, sex and sweat and latex and...me.

"Use your hands," he said, "guide me in."

Reaching down, I grasped his shaft. He hissed in a breath. "Easy with that, honey, I told you, it's primed to go off."

"Sorry." I loosened my grip.

"Nothing to be sorry about, you're just too sexy for your own good."

I glanced up at his face. A line of concentration had etched between his brows.

"Take me in," he murmured. "Take me into your sweet little body."

I shifted my hips as he lowered his pelvis toward me. The tip of his cock was so wide and big as I pressed it to my entrance. It didn't feel as if it would go in at all. It was like having the wrong key for a lock.

"Relax," he soothed. "Relax, Ashley, you know this can work."

"Yes," I said on a hot, panting breath as I forced my pelvic muscles to ease. "I know." I released his cock and held on to his bulging biceps.

He pushed forward, just an inch, sliding into my already wet channel. I gasped at the stretching and filling sensation he created in that first section of pussy. My nerves caught fire with excitement and anticipation. I was actually watching the moment of penetration. The very second I was about to say goodbye to my virginity. I couldn't speak. I could hardly breathe.

"You okay?"

"Mmm," I managed, staring at the rest of his shaft poised for penetration. It was so wide, so long—I suddenly wasn't so sure about this.

"Loosen up a bit more. Let it go, Ashley, you were designed for this, damn it, I think you were designed for me."

"Oh god," I groaned as he curled his coccyx under and gained another inch of invasion. "Oh, oh, I think that's enough." He'd filled me. I was stretched tight around his girth. I dug my fingernails into his skin. "No more."

"Not a chance," he muttered, the muscles in his arms shaking. "Still got a way to go yet, honey."

I brought my knees up to his hips and squeezed against him in an attempt to gain control, to slow him down, to stop him.

"Oh, those fucking stockings," he groaned, pushing in some more.

"Ah, ah, Shane I..." It was like a whip of fire inside me. I wasn't going to be able to take him all in. It was impossible.

"Shh, think about those books you read as research." His voice was strained. "Think about the virgins. They might have asked for it to stop but it doesn't, does it, not once it's started, not once it's got this far. It has to go on. Doesn't it, Ashley, tell me?"

"Yes, yes it does, I know, but this hurts. You said it wouldn't hurt."

"I'm sorry, I didn't think it would. I think you just need to relax. Let go of the tension inside."

"I'll try." I willed my pelvic muscles to soften.

"That's it, good girl," he said, dropping down so our chests connected. "You're doing so well and in about ten seconds it's going to be as perfect for you as it is for me."

He kissed me gently and rode into me, slow but firm. Filling me, possessing me, taking what he wanted.

I groaned around his kiss, pushing at his shoulders with my fists.

"Ashley, it's done, you've taken all of me, now just catch the spark again." He pulled out a fraction then rocked back in.

My body stiffened. As he'd rocked, his pubic bone had connected wonderfully with my clit.

"It's feeling better now, isn't it?" He repeated the action, rubbing me perfectly.

"Ah, yes, yes."

"It's so good for me too, so fucking good, you wouldn't believe."

"Shane," I gasped, pressing my hands to his cheeks and looping my ankles around the back of his thighs. "Yes, it's good." He was so high inside me, I was full and stretched. His cock was touching every part of me and pushing at my insides in a deeply satisfying invasion.

"God, I've never felt anything like you," he murmured, staring at my face. "You're tight and hot and sweet and you're gripping me so hard with your internal muscles it feels like you'll never let go."

"Hard, yes, hard," I said breathlessly, pushing his floppy hair from his face. "Please don't stop."

"Don't worry, I won't." He continued rocking. It was a graceful, gliding movement that rubbed my clit as he stroked his cock along my internal walls. He smiled, dropped his head and kissed me, pouring the taste of myself into my mouth along with his own divine masculine flavor. The pressure in my clit was growing again and I twitched my hips upward for more connection every time he smoothed into me.

"You want to go on top?" he asked, tracing his lips to my ear.

I didn't want to change a thing about what we were doing. I was on a ride to heaven.

"I think you'll like it." He didn't wait for me to answer. In one swift movement I was lifted upright over him with my legs bent at his sides. His cock hadn't left my pussy.

Gasping, I flattened my hands on his chest as my hair fell around my cheeks.

"Sit up," he said, wrapping his hands around my upper arms and holding me tight. "I want to see you ride me." He pushed me into a sitting position.

I froze. His cock was a thick, wide rod and I was *sitting* on it. He was so deep I was sure he was bumping into my cervix.

"Move, honey," he said, spreading his palms on the scalloped lace of my fishnets. "Move to catch all those hot spots." He urged me into a rocking rhythm.

Instantly my clit caught on his body again. His cock, so high, heightened the sensations tenfold. "Oh god, yes," I groaned, arching my back and tipping my head to the ceiling. "I like it like that, yes, yes, you were right, it's good on top."

"I know." He cupped my breasts and jerked his hips in time with my movements. I pressed my hands over his and encouraged him to tweak and pull at my nipples. I wanted sensations all over.

"Sweet Jesus," he muttered, pulling and teasing at both my nipples with his big, strong fingers.

I was going to climax again. I could feel it. Each time I rocked on him I was getting closer and closer. It felt amazing to be on top, female and sexy, empowering and erotic. I put my hands behind myself, rested them on his concrete thighs and jerked my pelvis, over and over, grinding, gyrating. I was fucking Shane, completely naked, he was hardly moving, it was all about me, riding him, crushing my clit against him and building up a wonderful orgasm.

"Oh shit, I hope you're close." I heard Shane mutter through the sound of blood racing in my ears.

"Yes, so near..."

Suddenly I was flat on my back again with a big, hungry man pressed over me.

"Now," he grunted fiercely, burying his face in my neck. "Come now, Ashley."

He gave one powerful ram and I split apart. An orgasm, big and intense, claimed my body, shaking me and twisting me inside out. "Shane, yes, ah, ah," I cried. "Oh, that's it." Every muscle in my body bucked and tensed. But I couldn't move, his weight on me was too heavy and tight.

"Fuck...ing...hell..." he moaned, lifting his head.

I tore open my eyes. He'd tipped his face back. The tendons on his neck were strained and his lips spread sideways in a tight grimace as he hissed in a long suck of air.

His chest pressed heavily on me as a long, pleasure-infused groan vibrated from him.

Finally his body stilled, though his breathing was erratic. "I'm sorry," he gasped into my ear.

"Why?" I asked breathlessly.

"I lost it a bit those last few seconds."

"It was amazing," I panted.

He smoothed back my hair as he took his weight onto his elbows. "Are you sure?" he asked. There were beads of sweat on his upper lip, catching in his stubble.

"Oh my god, yes, yes, everything and more than I thought it would be."

He dropped a light kiss to my lips. "Good, 'cause seeing you ride me, with no inhibitions, just taking what you wanted, was the sexiest damn thing I ever saw in my life."

Grinning, I lifted my head and kissed him, hot, hard and thoroughly. Inside I was dancing up and down, celebrating the loss of my damn virginity. It had been spectacular, carnal, utterly perfect.

"Oh, honey," he said, breaking the kiss. "I'm so going to have to go downstairs and empty that machine of condoms because there's no way once is enough, not with you."

His cock inside me had barely softened.

"Suits me," I said with a smile.

He withdrew, rolled off and dropped onto his back.

We lay side by side, breathless and sweaty, staring at the tartan canopy over the bed.

Chapter Five

"I think I might take a shower," I said after a few minutes. My skin was cooling and I'd become aware of a damp tackiness between my legs.

He turned his head and grinned. "Want company?"

"Mm, that would be another first."

He twitched his eyebrows and stood. "Well, we'll have to make it count then." He reached for my hand, tugged me to standing and led me to the bathroom.

Within seconds the huge shower cubicle was filled with hot, swirling steam. I slipped off my stockings and we stepped under the torrent of water. Drawing me close, he set about kissing me, lazily, indulgently as the water soaked over our hair and bodies. Gently, he nibbled down my neck and across my collarbone while exploring my back and butt with his hands.

The feel of a hot, wet body pressed against mine in the shower was divine. He was hard and slippery, and the hairs on his forearms, chest and abdomen as they brushed across my sensitive skin, utterly delicious.

"You have a great bum," he said, cupping a butt cheek in each palm and squeezing.

"Thanks," I giggled.

"Just the right size for me to grope." He grinned and continued to massage. Buzzing sensations traveled to my pussy, his enjoyment of my rear a total turn-on.

He furrowed his brow. "Damn, I should have got those condoms before I jumped in this shower with you. We could have found your other sweet spot in here and I could have worshipped your butt while it was all wet and slippery."

Lust screamed through me again, his words an aphrodisiac all on their own. God, I wanted him in me again, burying fast and hard from behind, finding my G-spot, making me cry out with pleasure. "So go, go and get some," I said, blinking water from my eyes.

"I will in a minute." He reached for the hand attachment of the shower. "Once I've made sure your first shared shower is memorable."

I stared at his handsome face as he adjusted the water setting on the attachment, making the stream hard and fast. If I never had a shower with another guy in my life I would be quite happy. He needed to do nothing other than just stand there naked, wet and gorgeous and it was perfect. He was so damn sexy, how could anyone else ever compare?

"Like this," he said, backing me up until my shoulders hit smooth, cool tiles.

He blasted the jet into his palm then reached for my hand and did the same to me. It tickled in a strong, vibrating way. I curled my fist around the spray.

"Do you trust me?"

I nodded.

"Then go with it, just enjoy." He pulled my arm straight and moved the jet of water up the inside of my forearm, over the delicate underside of my elbow and onto my shoulder. My sensitive skin greedily lapped up the pounding sensation.

What is he doing?

He moved the jet down my collarbone and onto the top rise of my breast, watching his movements carefully.

My breasts felt heavy with desire, my nipples had puckered. The stream of beating water moved lower, then circled my areola.

"Shane," I gasped, holding on to his wrist. The hard sensation was new and deep.

"Shh," he soothed, keeping the jet perfectly still so that it pounded relentlessly at my nipple. "Does it feel nice?"

"Yes, different, but yes, nice." I pinched my other nipple, twisting it between my fingers and tugging until pain mixed with the sensations.

He smiled as though again enjoying my uninhibited actions. "It's going to feel even nicer down here." The water moved downward, over my ribs and navel. "Open your legs, honey, and you should lock your knees."

My mind spun as I realized what he was going to do. "I-I don't know."

"It's okay," he said, kissing me gently. "I can't make you come with my cock until I've stocked up on condoms, but you'll like this way of climaxing, I'm sure of it."

I parted my legs as the beating water pounded over my pubic hair. Still I kept hold of his wrist. The jet was so strong, so forceful, and I needed to have some control as it went near my most delicate flesh.

He glanced down, his black eyelashes heavy with drips. Using his free hand, he parted my folds to reveal my pale, still-swollen clit.

"So pretty," he murmured.

The water hit.

"Ah!" I went up on my tiptoes and shifted away.

"Stay with it," he said. "You'll come fast and hard, just stay with it."

"It's too much." I shook my head and writhed against the tiles.

He grinned and pressed his legs to mine, pinning me in place. "You said that last time and ended up having a wild ride, remember?"

I swallowed. He was right. I wanted to do as he asked, really I did.

"Ashley," he murmured onto my lips. "Trust me to make you feel good."

The water was back, hammering through my pubic hair. I nodded, sucking in a hot, wet breath and bracing for it hitting my delicate clit again.

This time I forced myself not to move as it connected. "Oh god," I groaned into his mouth. The sensation was so intense, so concentrated.

"Come," he murmured. "Come again, beautiful lady."

Already my orgasm was growing and suddenly the thought of moving away from the water pressure was unthinkable. It felt fabulous, amazing. The strong stimulation direct and focused, building me up so quickly my head spun and my muscles trembled.

"Shane," I gasped, clutching his shoulder for support. "I'm going to..."

"I know, take it."

I was floating, nothing existed except for Shane directing hammering water at my clit. I shut my eyes, started to call out but no sound emerged. The plane of bliss I was on was vibrant and all-consuming.

Then my pussy was clamping down, spasming around nothing, and my clit exploded in ecstatic, throbbing pulsations.

"Ah god, yes, yes, please, no more."

The shower attachment fell to the floor, freeing my clit of the wicked water. He kissed me, hard, pulling me into his body.

My knees would barely hold me and I clung to him as my whole pelvis contracted over and over. I gasped at the speed and ferocity he'd brought me to climax with his naughty little trick. I was hot and feverish and aware of sweat pricking over my body even though I was standing beneath a shower of water.

"I told you to trust me," he said, nipping my bottom lip lightly then trailing kisses to the hollow of my throat. "I know my way around a woman's body, and yours is just about the sweetest and most responsive I've ever had the pleasure of exploring."

Fluttering my eyes shut, I reveled in his delicate kisses and his raw strength. "Keep exploring, I like it."

He chuckled, reaching for the shower gel and filling his palms with the spicy ginger liquid. With a quick rub of his hands it turned to white foam. "Turn around, honey."

I did as he instructed and he coated my back in suds, creeping his hands 'round to slide over my breasts and down between my legs. "How did you?" I paused. "I mean how do you know something like that?"

His lips were by my ear. "What do you mean?"

"How did you know the water would make me come so fast?"

"You really want to know?"

I nodded.

He sighed. "I surprised Mandy in the shower once. She was squatted on the floor getting herself off with the hard stream of water from the mobile attachment."

"Oh." I pictured his ex-wife, beautiful I was sure, masturbating in the shower as she waited for him to join her and start the real thing. "I see."

He tweaked my soapy nipples. "We'd just made love. I guess she'd faked it and headed off to the shower to find her release."

Faked it? With Shane?

It was unthinkable. I could orgasm again just from him rubbing suds on my breasts. The woman had something seriously wrong with her.

I turned to face him and the water washed away the bubbles on my chest. "Well, I'm sorry if that made you feel bad, which I'm sure it did, but I'm not sorry you discovered that unique shower experience for me to enjoy." I kissed him and his hard cock strained against my belly.

"Mm," he murmured. "I'm glad it worked so well." He probed his tongue into my mouth and tangled it with mine, slid his hands down my back and onto my butt. "Ah, fuck." He pulled away from our wet, rapidly intensifying kiss. "If I don't get outta here now and go get those condoms, you, Ashley, could find yourself the mother of my child." He pulled away and grinned broadly. "I'll be back in ten minutes, go get some rest. You'll need it."

I stared at his broad, water-coated back as he stepped quickly from the shower and grabbed a huge white towel. Within seconds he was striding from the steamy bathroom and I was alone.

I held my face up to the water and closed my eyes.

The mother of his child?

It wasn't an abhorrent thought, not by a long shot. He was the perfect man as far as I was concerned. Not just successful and handsome and charming like all the heroes from my novels, but also wickedly sexy and real, so real, with history and demons and ambitions for the future. Everything about him was fascinating, from his slightly crooked smile to his groans of pleasure when he'd come. His butt and back were adorable, his hands and his fingertips as they touched me were gentle and skillful.

My belly clenched at the memory of my three wonderful orgasms and at the thought of more to come.

Get some rest, you'll need it.

Running my hands over my body, I gently touched my no longer virginal pussy. My clit was still sensitive and swollen, my entrance tender. But it felt the same, only now it felt like Shane's, if just for one night.

I'd given him a part of me. But it was more than my virginity, I sensed that already. I'd given him a part of my history, of my life as a woman. I had given him a key to my soul and a slice of my heart.

After drying and slathering exotic-scented lotion over my body, I pulled on the luxurious hotel robe and flopped on the bed. The room was quiet and still without

Shane, and I decided to indulge in a few pages from my favorite e-book while I waited for him to return.

Stolen and Seduced. Just the title had me tingling with anticipation. The way misunderstood gangster Hest had snatched upper-class Eliza Winters from the restroom of The Plaza was so sinfully sexy. He'd held her captive in his hotel room. Tied her to a bed and slowly, erotically forced her to admit her feelings for him, admit that she loved him despite the social implications of their union. It was all so toe-curlingly bad. He'd been inventive with his ways of torturing her sweetly and all the time she'd bubbled with pleasure and fallen even more in love with him, despite her anger and frustration.

I flicked to halfway through.

Eliza's wrists ached. She had been bound for forty-eight hours now, gagged some of the time, naked all of it. She knew every nook and cranny on the ceiling, every silver fleur-de-lis on the elegant duck-egg wallpaper.

She licked her lips, grateful for the lack of panties in her mouth, for that was what Hest used when he wanted to be sure she didn't cry out.

Turning, she saw the knife on the bedside table. It was early morning, she was sure of it. The light seeping through the crack in the heavy cord curtains was weak but hinted at dawn. Hest was awake in the armchair, he rarely slept. But she'd known this about him for a long time, she believed this was one of the reasons he obsessed about things, obsessed about her. He had more time to dwell than normal people, more hours in his day.

His piercing blue eyes settled on hers, and without a word he stood and held a cup of water to her lips. Eliza swallowed gratefully, her mouth still salty from the semen she'd sucked from his cock a few hours ago.

A trickle of water ran down her chin and he caught it on the pad of his thumb and drew it to his own lips. After taking it into his mouth he asked, "Are you ready to admit what you feel for me?"

Eliza shook her head and tried to cross her legs but couldn't. She remembered that her ankles were also tethered to the bedposts. Her poor, ravished pussy was exposed to the cool air and available for him to tease to the point of climax then leave her hanging whenever he wanted. Whenever the mood took him.

"Hest," she pleaded. "You know it could never work between us, we're too different, what you are asking of me is pointless."

"No, it isn't," he growled, "don't say that." A muscle in his jaw flexed and relaxed. Eliza knew this was not a good sign.

I snuggled my head down on the pillow and flicked forward a couple of pages, wanting to skip their discussion about how he could make things work for them. Hest had it all figured out, Eliza just needed to give herself up to him. I adored Hest now. The first time I'd read the book I'd been unsure, but now I knew the ending, his drastic actions and raw determination were all the more appealing.

Yawning loudly, I carried on reading.

Eliza didn't know if she could take another ride to the brink of orgasm. Hest had been teasing and tormenting her at the edge of ecstasy for so long, it was a dark, desperate pleasure so intense, so extreme that she didn't know if her heart could physically take it.

He kissed her again, roughly, savagely as his hips pounded. His cock was so deep, so hard, despite the fact he had climaxed several times in the last few hours. It was as though he would never get enough of her, like he wanted to get inside of her, be a part of her. She knew how he felt, it was how she felt, she could admit it to herself, but what was the point of admitting it to him? They could never be together.

"Hest," she cried around his mouth when he suddenly stopped just as she was about to come. "Please. Why are you torturing us both like this?"

"Say it," he growled. "Say you love me, say you'll be mine for all of time."

Eliza screwed up her eyes, bit down on her lip, tasted blood. She clamped her pussy muscles around him and shifted her hips, desperate for more pressure on her clit.

He withdrew and shimmied down her body, dragged at the knots on her ankles and the next thing she knew, he'd flipped her onto her stomach, her cheek squashed into the soft pillow and her large breasts flattened beneath her. "Mmff, Hest...what are you doing?" she managed as her forearms crossed over one another.

"You are one damn stubborn lady but you met your match when you met me," he whispered harshly into her ear. "You should never have taken me up on that drink six months ago. Chatting to strangers in dark bars after midnight will only get you into trouble."

Boy, was that a truth if ever Eliza had heard one.

He wrapped his hands around her hips and forged into her from behind. The head of his cock pounded against her G-spot, tunneling in deeper than she could ever imagine he'd go.

She cried out at the mix of pain/pleasure and he quickly released her right hip and clamped his hand over mouth.

"Keep it quiet, my darling," he growled, his breath hot and hard in her ear. "We don't want anyone to raise an alarm and spoil our fun, not when I have this room booked out for the next two weeks if need be."

Eliza whimpered as an orgasm sped toward her again. She needed it so badly. He had to let her take it this time. Because two weeks of this erotic torture, of not being allowed to come but being within reach of ecstasy, oh god, she would surely die of frustration.

My body was heavy with exhaustion, my eyelids a struggle to keep open. Shane had been gone longer than I thought. I shrugged off the robe and slipped my legs beneath the covers, it was warm and cozy and the sheets were made of the finest cotton.

"Say it and I'll let you orgasm. I know how much you like it like this, Eliza, only I know, only I truly understand what your horny little body needs. Only I can give you what you need for the rest of your life."

Eliza opened her mouth behind his hand, the words sat heavy on her tongue. They were the truth, she loved him, she could hold it in no longer. "Yes," she said in a muffled voice. "Yes, Hest, I do."

His hand lifted and his lips pressed onto her ear. "Say it," he growled, pulling his cock out and thrusting back in. Farther than ever before and drawing the orgasm tantalizingly within reach.

"Yes, Hest, I love you. I love you so much."

"And you want me, you want to be my wife." His voice was strained and his body a slab of solid concrete over her.

"Yes, I want to be your wife, yes, please, let me come, I'm yours."

"Forever?"

"Yes, forever."

Their shout of combined ecstasy rang around the room, rattling the glass chandelier and echoing into the bathroom. Eliza gave herself up to every spasm and tremor Hest tore from her. Absorbed every pounding jerk of his body, knowing that she was no longer lying to herself. She had been stubborn, she had even been foolish. There was no denying they were made for one another. Hest was the only man who made her crazy with lust, drunk with desire and loopy with love.

*****

"Hey, sleepyhead."

I peeled open my eyes. Shane sat in bed next to me, propped up on pillows and sipping from a white mug. He had my ereader on his knees.

"Did you sleep well?" He grinned. "Not that I need to ask, you were out like a light when I got back and apart from a few cute little murmurs and twitches you barely moved all night."

Glancing at the digital clock—8:39—I wriggled upright. "Sorry," I said, pushing a hand through my hair. It must look shocking. It had been damp when I'd gone to bed.

He leaned over and pressed a coffee-infused kiss to my lips. "Don't be sorry," he whispered. "You had a busy evening." He smiled. "And I'm sure we'll make use of some of these condoms before we have to check out."

My heart sank. Shit. Of course. It was morning, which meant my one-night stand was over.

How could I have fallen asleep and wasted that sexy, once-in-a-lifetime opportunity?

"I bumped into Derek in the restroom," Shane said, rubbing his index finger over his dark stubble. "He caught me in the act of emptying all my pound coins into the machine."

There was a slight rise of color on Shane's cheeks as he nodded at three boxes of condoms on the dresser. The top pack read, "Ribbed For Her Pleasure".

"Oh," I said. "And...?"

"After giving me the weirdest look he said he needed to talk to me, that he would call me over the holidays." Shane put down his coffee and turned to me. "Would he be pissed that we hooked up?"

I shook my head. "No, I don't think so. But how would he know it was me you were buying those for?"

Shane grinned. "Because last time he saw you, honey, he'd just passed you into my arms."

"Oh, yes." I smiled as memories of dancing with Shane flooded my mind. It had been wonderful, so had afterward, back here. "I guess he's a bit protective of me. I've worked there since I was eighteen. We're good friends, but I'm sure it's nothing, he probably wants to chat to you about Safe as Houses."

"Mmm, yeah, probably." Shane sighed, got out of bed and, gloriously naked, strolled to the desk where a kettle was set with cups and condiments. "You want coffee?"

I stared at his pert butt and long lean back, desperately hoping he'd start getting his money's worth out of those condoms soon—we had only a couple of hours until checkout.

"Er, yes, please, coffee would be great." Tearing my gaze from his backside, I glanced at the ereader. It was on the second-to-last page of *Stolen and Seduced*.

My breath hitched.

Oh damn, did I leave it on?

"Have you been awake long?" I asked.

"Yeah, ages, I couldn't sleep after seeing Derek, my mind was whirring, plus I didn't want to miss out if you happened to wake up."

"And what have you been doing, while I was out for the count?"

He turned and the sinewy muscles beneath the skin on his back stretched and pulled taut. "I've been reading."

I gulped. "What? I...um..what have you been reading?" Surely not my erotic romance stories, surely not *Stolen and Seduced*. I would die of embarrassment. What would he think of my taste in raunchy fiction?

"Whatever it was you'd been reading before you fell asleep. I hit 'beginning' and read the whole thing, well, apart from the last couple of pages but I can pretty much figure out the end now." He held up a sachet of sugar.

I shook my head and tugged the duvet up over my naked breasts.

"It's a great book," he said, walking over with the steaming mug.

I tried to avert my eyes from his semi-erect cock, unsure of what "morning-after-the-night-before" etiquette was.

"The guy was a rough diamond, wasn't he? I wasn't sure to start with if Eliza really liked him or not, but it was well written the way she kept having flashbacks to their previous meetings, and how she knew she was falling for him even though she didn't want to. It was really clever."

Taking the coffee he handed me, I nodded.

Shane slipped back into bed, his face full of enthusiasm. "And I loved the hotel room they were in. It was a bit like this one." He glanced around. "Well, maybe a bit more modern but the story could almost have been set here, couldn't it?"

"Mmm, yeah, I guess." I sipped my coffee, surprised by Shane's apparent enjoyment of my "girly" book.

"And it was hot, blimey, there were no descriptions left out and that author has one hell of an imagination, doesn't he?"

"She."

"Sorry, she."

I smiled. "You really enjoyed it?"

He took my coffee and set it aside. When his gaze caught mine, his eyes were sparkling. "Yeah, probably a bit too much, it's made me horny as hell."

In one swift movement, he dragged me down the bed and plonked on top of me. I gasped as his mouth connected with mine and his now very hard cock nudged at my thigh. "So if it is okay with you, Ashley," he whispered, peppering kisses over my lips and onto my cheek, "I'm going to make sweet, morning love to you and savor every tiny whimper and gasp your delectable body produces."

"Sounds like a great plan," I murmured, wrapping my legs around the back of his thighs. My pussy was already wet for him, my nipples tingling as they pressed up against his hairy pectoral muscles.

"Just let me reach one of those condoms." He stretched sideways. Fiddled with a pack then sat back on his heels, the duvet bunching around his butt. He tore the wrapper and rolled the condom down the length of his shaft. It was red latex and the color made his erection appear all the more flushed, angry almost. He glanced at me watching. "Don't worry, I'm sure we'll have time to use a ribbed one if you want that experience too."

Nodding, because I certainly did want that experience, I hoped I'd still be able to accommodate his girth in the light of day. Last night I'd been softened by champagne and high on lust. Not that I wasn't high on lust now, I just prayed that we would still fit.

"Relax, honey," he murmured, leaning over me, fisting his cock and directing it at my spread pussy. "You know how great it feels when I'm inside you, just let me in." He pushed his hips forward and entered me an inch.

Gasping, I fluttered my eyes shut and willed myself to let him penetrate me. He was so damn big, so damn hard. Just the head of his cock made me feel full and tight.

"Just imagine Eliza taking Hest for that first time back in the hotel room," he said in a strained voice. "She wanted it so bad, and even though she wouldn't admit it he knew how much she needed them to join, and so to help her he just did this." As Shane spoke he forged slowly but determinedly forward.

"Ah, ow...Shane," I cried, gripping his shoulders.

"Eliza takes it all," he ground out. "Every bit of Hest and he adores her for that doesn't he? Loves the fact that she wants him so much even though it hurts at first."

"Yes, yes, oh yes." My pussy was gradually expanding, allowing his entry. And I was so wet, how had I gotten so wet for him so fast? It was

like a tap had been turned on, my body reacting to his so basically and
without cognitive thought.

He hooked his hand beneath my thigh, drew it upward so my knee
touched above his hip and buried himself to the hilt. My sharp cry pe-
tered into a groan of edgy pleasure.

"Oh, honey, you feel so good," he said, withdrawing and smoothing
back in, expertly catching my clit.

"Oh god, so do you." I slotted my fingers into his messy hair and
held his face firm for a kiss. I needed to show him with my mouth, my
tongue, how good he made me feel, how wonderful every tiny thing he
did was, even if I gasped and whimpered.

He set up a perfect, steady rhythm, sliding in and out. Each time he
hit maximum penetration, a little jolt of air shunted from my lungs. I
could stay like this forever, with Shane inside me, loving me, showing
me the way to heavenly bliss. He was the air that I breathed, everything
in my vision was him. The beat of his heart vibrating against mine was
the perfect, synchronized tempo. We were so connected, joined as one
being. I needed nothing else, ever.

"Did the story turn you on too?" Shane asked breathily. "When
you read it.

I hesitated, struggling for coherent words. "Yes, yes it did."

"Which parts?"

"I-I don't know."

Is this really a time for conversation?

"Yes you do, tell me." He stilled, buried as deep as he could go. "Tell
me, Ashley, which pages made you feel hot and bothered and dampened your knickers?"

I stared into his piercing gaze, felt as though I was looking into his
soul and him into mine. I could only be honest. "I guess when she was
first taken, when she knew it was the man she loved and who loved
her but at the same time he was unpredictable..." I paused as my pussy

clamped around his cock, relishing the fact he was so deep, so big and so hard inside me.

"Oh fuck," he groaned. "Go on."

"Unpredictable and, and dangerous, she didn't think he'd hurt her but with a knife at her throat and the mood he was in it could go either way."

Shane began to move again, building me up to bliss. "And you liked how he tied her up, teased her, used her for his own pleasure but denied her an orgasm."

"Yes, yes, oh god, yes, I liked it. Please, don't stop."

"I won't but tell me, tell me, if I do this." Suddenly he grabbed my wrists and yanked them above my head, pressed them hard into the pillow.

I grunted as his full weight hit my chest for a brief moment. Then he loomed above me, harnessing me beneath him. A new wave of exhilaration washed through me, I didn't think I could feel any more turned-on but suddenly, again, I was dizzy with excitement.

"You're mine," he grunted, his eyes flashing. "You can go nowhere. Like Eliza, you're trapped, my hostage, and I'm going to enjoy your body, take my pleasure."

His handsome face twisted with dominance, power bled from his fingers into my wrists.

He hammered in and out, faster and faster as I clenched and bucked beneath him. My clit was being battered against his body, swelling and pulsing, taking everything he had to offer.

My climax claimed me. "Oh, oh, Shane, oh please, yes, that's it."

I peeled open my eyes, not wanting to miss a thing, watching as he arched his neck to the ceiling. "Fuck, what the hell are you doing to me?" he groaned, forcing his hips harder than ever between my inner thighs. It was as though he wouldn't be happy until he penetrated my diaphragm.

I couldn't catch my breath, it was fast and wheezing. I was flying high, my hands, my body surrendered to Shane. His words, spoken in passion, were embedded in my ears, his face contorted with ecstasy now imprinted on my mind's eye. He was the other half of me. Sparks flew between us, the heavens collided—we were destined for this moment.

"Oh, sweet Jesus," he groaned, dropping his head to my neck. "That was awesome."

"Yes." I pulled on my arms and he immediately released me, allowing me to wrap my hands around his shoulders and hold him tight. He scooped his forearms beneath my shoulders and pulled me close, holding me against his hot body as he panted.

We stayed locked together and catching our breath for a long time. Eventually his cock softened and he lifted up, sliding from me.

My stomach growled.

He laughed and tugged off the condom. "I guess I ought to feed you. All that activity before breakfast has made you hungry."

Smiling, I stretched my arms above my head again, adoring the comfortable way I could be with him, naked and satisfied. "Mmm, I guess you should, Mr. Closet Dominant."

His face lit. "You," he grinned, "are a naughty little virgin who shouldn't know about all this stuff, and certainly shouldn't enjoy it as much as you do."

"I think we can safely say I'm no longer a virgin, and I told you, I read a lot."

He bent and kissed me lightly. "I like the stuff you read, it's sexy as hell and yes, you're right about the fact you're definitely not a virgin anymore." He paused. "And, honey, I will never, ever forget our night together. It's been and still is, wonderful."

Chapter Six

Shane reached for the phone and ordered breakfast in the room. I showered, quickly and alone, and pulled on the robe as he flicked through the news channels. It seemed the snow over the entire UK had been relentless overnight—three feet deep in places with drifts up to six feet.

Breakfast arrived, a fabulous spread of smoked salmon, eggs and fresh fruit, another pot of coffee and a basket of croissants and Danish pastries. I tucked in eagerly as Shane reached for a white envelope balanced against two glasses of freshly squeezed orange juice.

"What's that?" I asked.

He read it with a serious expression then looked up at me and grinned. "It seems the hotel is advising guests to avoid travel. The lane to the nearest main road is impassable."

I cocked my head and nibbled on a slice of melon.

"They're offering a fifty percent discount to stay tonight. No one coming in, no one going out, they're as stuck with us as we are with them."

My heart flipped with hope.

Is my one-night stand about to turn into a two-night stand?

He smiled. "So what do you reckon? Am I invited to stay in your lavish suite or should I head down to my own small, standard room?"

Excitement zipped through me. He was asking to stay here, with me, another night. I couldn't help thinking that some beautiful angel was smiling down on me and rewarding me for being such a good girl for all of those years. "Stay here," I said quickly. "No point in paying for two rooms when this one is perfectly big and comfortable for us both."

"Are you sure? People might talk."

I shrugged. "Only if they find out, and so what if they do? We're both single, both entitled to spend time together."

He nodded slowly. "Okay, but just so we're clear, it's not the room that's making me want to stay here." He leaned over and popped a slice of strawberry into my mouth. "It's the person hanging out and looking like the most delicious part of my breakfast that's tempted me."

He kissed me, a strawberry-infused kiss that made my heart sing.

Shane went to collect his stuff and I dressed in my jeans and sweater. When he returned he too was in jeans. He also wore a hooded top with a Manchester United logo on the right side of his chest.

"You a fan?" I asked.

"No other team worth supporting." He grinned and dropped his holdall to the floor. "Shall we head down to reception, sort out the room, I'll get the bill. Then maybe we could take a walk, the snow's spectacular."

"Sounds good."

"Because," he said, winding his fingers with mine, "there's no rush now to try out those ribbed condoms and we have a whole other night to make sure we find that sweet little spot of yours."

A flush traveled over my cheeks. Having him speak of my G-spot in the harsh light of day reminded me how wanton I'd been in declaring what I wanted and, of course, what I'd already done.

He laughed and pressed a kiss to my temple. Scooped up the key and tugged me out of the room.

As Shane sorted the tab for the suite, I wandered into the small hotel gift shop opposite the reception desk. It was early and there was hardly anyone about. It seemed not having to check out had made everyone lazy.

I fingered a cashmere scarf with the hotel logo embroidered on it and checked the price on a gorgeous emerald-green sweater. I would never normally have considered such a vibrant color. But having worn my new red dress last night, it seemed more of a possibility .

I spotted a row of navy wellington boots in a variety of sizes. Glanced at my sneakers then out the lead-paned window at the drifts of snow sparkling in the sunlight. I couldn't walk in the snow in sneakers, my feet would be wet through in no time. Come to think of it, neither could Shane.

Quickly, I slipped into the boots. They fit beautifully, the inside lined with fleece and the base padded.

"Hey, pretty lady," Shane said, coming up behind me and winding a hand around my waist. "You'll need them for wandering around the hotel grounds."

I leaned into him and rested my hands on his forearms. It was wonderful the way our bodies were so comfortable with each other. "Yes, much better than those." I nodded at my discarded sneakers. "I'll treat us both to a pair since you paid for the room."

He released me and searched out his size. "No, I'll get them."

"Let me." I took the boots he'd chosen, glanced at the girl behind the till and lowered my voice. "Plus you bought the mountain of condoms."

He touched the tip of his finger to the rise of my cheekbone. "Money well spent," he whispered.

I gazed into his eyes. They were dark and heavy. I recognized the swirling depth they took on when he was thinking or speaking about sex. And to know he was thinking and talking about sex with me was such a turn-on it made my pulse rate soar and I'm sure caused my own eyes to sparkle with lust.

"Okay, you get the boots," he said. "And I'll get you that scarf you were looking at."

I raised my eyebrows.

"You think I took my eyes off you when I was at the desk? Not a chance. While we're here, you're mine, and I am going to savor every moment."

While we're here I'm his.

The words settled in my chest like a warm caress. I loved being Shane's. I adored being here at The Fenchurch with him.

The thought of our time together ending was too painful to contemplate so I shoved it from my mind with barely a falter in my smile.

After donning boots and coats we headed outside. The Cotswolds had been transformed into a winter wonderland. Fields of snow covering shrubs and hedgerows surrounded the hotel. A few tall copses in the distance peeked out at a crystal blue sky and the cars in the parking lot were hardly visible.

Sucking in the sharp clear air, I squinted at the brightness and snuggled my chin into my new scarf. Shane linked his gloved fingers with mine and we headed along a semi-clear path toward the back of the hotel.

The fresh snow squeaked beneath my new boots and the cold nipped my cheeks.

"I haven't seen this much snow in years," Shane said.

"I know, it's beautiful. In London it only stays white for a few hours and then it turns to gray slush."

"I haven't been to London since the summer. I went with a few mates on a stag weekend."

"Was it good?"

"Yeah, awesome."

We rounded the corner of the hotel, our breath misting in front of us. "Have you always lived in London?" he asked.

"Yes, I grew up in Muswell Hill but now I'm just off Portobello."

"Nice."

"Yes, it is." I thought of my little flat. It was a bit old-fashioned. The carpet could do with replacing as could some of the clanging radiators. But it was home. It was my space in the world and I loved it.

"Perhaps I could call in next time I'm in the city."

I stopped and turned to him. My heart rate picked up and my mind spun. Maybe tomorrow morning wasn't the end of us after all.

He grinned and pulled me close. "Would I be pushing the boundaries of whatever this is we're doing if I got your cell number?"

"Shane, I—"

His lips brushed mine. "I guess I'm not much good at one-night stands, and two-nights stands even worse." His eyebrows pulled low, his expression turned serious. "Ashley, I'm going to want to spend more time with you. I know it's hard us living so far apart, but..." His voice trailed off.

"But maybe we could try," I finished for him.

He grinned. "Yes, maybe we could try." He stroked his gloved palm down my hair and cupped my cold cheek. "Because I haven't felt like this for a long time."

I sucked in a breath. "And how do you feel?" I hardly dared ask for fear the words I hoped he would say wouldn't be uttered.

"Comfortable and excited all at the same time." He smoothed his other hand to my butt and squeezed me closer. "Completely fascinated by another person and feeling like I will never, ever get enough."

My heart tripped over itself and I gasped as the steely length of his erection made contact with my hipbone even through our layers of clothing.

"Shit, and I'm so damn horny all the time. I suggested a walk because I thought you needed a break from bedroom action." He pulled a face as if he was in real, physical pain and shifted his stance.

"I was doing just fine."

"I know, honey, but I didn't want that to change and it would on a forty-eight hour sex marathon." He glanced about and a naughty grin tugged at his mouth. "Although I could always drag you behind one of those trees and introduce you to *al fresco* sex if you want."

I giggled and clung to the lapels of his jacket. The naughty suggestion was actually quite tempting—for a split second—then I thought of frostbite on my butt. "A bit cold for that, don't you think?"

"Yeah, I guess." His gaze captured mine and his face fell serious. "You have the most beautiful eyes."

I blinked and looked away.

"Ashley." He used the crook of his finger to turn me to face him again. "Don't, I want to study them in this light."

I stared up into his dark, heavy gaze as he looked into mine. It was as though we were really looking at each other. Honestly, nothing in between. With anyone else I would have turned, shy, but not with Shane. Shane was different. Already he knew me like no one else did. He was with me, had been inside me, my head, my books and my body. Shane had claimed more of me than anyone else ever had or would be able to again.

"Your eyes are such an unusual shade of green," he murmured. "Like pine trees, but with little chocolate chips in them."

I smiled. "And yours are such a dark brown that it's hard to tell the difference between the pupil and iris. A bit like a puddle of treacle or a new road just covered with tarmac." I looked at his long lashes, the type of thick curls most girls would give their right arm for.

He grinned then kissed me, gently, just dipping his tongue into my mouth, the bristles on his chin scraping my cool skin. I clung to him as a scary new emotion ballooned in my chest, threatening to steal my breath and weaken my legs. Surely I wasn't falling in love with him. Not this quickly. No way.

"Hey, you two."

We pulled apart, though Shane kept an arm tight around my waist. I turned to see Rachel and Jeremy heading our way hand in hand. They too had purchased wellington boots and were well wrapped against the bitter cold.

"Hi," Shane said, his breath misting. "Bonus extra day, eh."

"Yep, the weather couldn't have timed it better for us. And half-price rooms too." Rachel smiled and looked between us. "You two hit it off at the party then."

"She put me under a spell," Shane said, grinning down at me.

"I'm not surprised you fell for it, Shane. Ashley, you looked divine in that red dress last night, it really suited you."

I wanted to say something to the tune of "oh, the dress wasn't mine," or "what, that old thing?" but I didn't, instead I smiled and said, "Thanks."

"Mmm, she did look divine, didn't she," Shane agreed, squeezing me a little closer.

"We're going to walk to The Three Horseshoes, apparently it's just across this field on a back lane," Jeremy said, nodding over the glittering field of snow. "It says in the brochure they do a top rate cottage pie."

"That and the thought of a log fire and a glass of merlot is enough to make me battle snowdrifts." Rachel grinned. "Why don't you join us?"

Shane turned to me. "What do you reckon?"

"It sounds lovely," I said. "By the time we walk there we will have built up our appetites again."

He raised his eyebrows, just a fraction, and I knew that if Rachel and Jeremy hadn't been standing there he would have made a comment about appetites of a different kind.

"That's settled then," he said. "Let's head for The Three Horseshoes."

It took forty minutes of stomping to reach the old stone public house and by the time we arrived I was hot beneath my layers of clothes. "This is so pretty," I said, looking up. The thatched roof was practically hidden beneath a thick blanket of snow and a snake of gray smoke trailed upward from the chimney.

We stamped the snow from our boots in a small porch then ducked into the low-beamed bar area. The landlord greeted us and launched into tales of snow chaos as he poured our drinks. There were few other customers and we guessed most people had stayed indoors. We didn't mind, it meant we didn't have to fight for the best table—the one near the roaring log fire and the lavishly decorated Christmas tree.

Rachel sat opposite me and as the men went to the bar to order our food she leaned forward. "He's had a really rough year, you know."

"Shane?"

She nodded.

"He told me," I said. "About the divorce."

Rachel shook her head and glanced over at Shane. He was standing with his back to us and I couldn't help but admire his tight butt and long, lean legs perfectly showcased in dark denim.

"Mandy was such a cow about everything—wanted the house, the car and all their savings. The woman has no integrity whatsoever, she's such a bitch."

I took a sip of my rich red wine.

"And of course it was all her fault, what with her carrying on with Jared. But Shane being Shane, he just wanted her gone, he didn't care about the financial cost. It was over and he wanted his life and his pride back. I missed him when he dashed off to Australia like that."

I tipped my head for her to go on.

She reached forward and placed her hand on my forearm. "Oh no, nothing like that, we're just friends, good friends. I missed having him in the office, making me laugh, sorting out all my day-to-day technology disasters, of which there are many."

I smiled and she sat back and reached for her own drink. The flickering shadows of the fire danced across her pretty face and reflected in her glasses. Her expression became serious once more. "Just be careful with him, okay? He hasn't dated since his divorce. He's a soft soul and I'd hate to see him hurt again. I don't know how well he'd bounce back."

There was no way I'd hurt Shane; in a few short hours he'd become one of the most important people in my life.

"But one thing is for sure, Ashley, you've certainly brought a smile to his face and a twinkle to his eye. It's great to see the old Shane again."

Her words made *me* smile and I glanced over at him once more. He was laughing at something the barman was saying, his head tipped back and his hands shoved in his front pockets. If I'd made him feel good again and able to laugh, then he'd made me feel as though I'd landed in heaven. He'd allowed me to be the hot-blooded woman I was for the first time in my life. He was so much more than a one-night stand and thank goodness we were going to be seeing each other again, making a go of it between London and Huddersfield. Maybe soon I would even be able to call him my boyfriend.

The thought sent a thrilling tingle up my spine. Shane Galloway, my boyfriend. Whoever would have thought the office mouse would get so monumentally lucky?

The meal was fantastic and well worth the walk. The landlord made the cottage pie himself and served it still wearing his blue-and-white striped apron. It seemed none of his staff had turned up for work but it didn't worry him since the pub was so quiet and he was a jack-of-all-trades.

The conversation between the four of us flowed easy and light. Rachel and Jeremy seemed well matched and very comfortable with each other. Jeremy even went as far as spooning chunks of his chocolate torte into Rachel's mouth.

It was cozy by the fire and after a few glasses of wine and sitting within the curve of Shane's arm I began to feel my mood soften to one of utter contentment. "I could stay here forever."

"Me too, but we ought to get going," Jeremy said, nodding out the window at the darkening sky. "It's nearly the shortest day, the light will soon be gone and there's no streetlamps around here to show us the way back."

Shane sighed and stood. "Yep, I guess you're right, although I have to say, this has been a wonderful afternoon."

I nodded in agreement and stood. Shane reached for my coat and scarf and helped me on with them before shrugging into his own.

The trudge back was swifter than the journey to the pub. We were all conscious of getting caught in the dark, but fortunately it wasn't long before we spotted the welcoming golden lights of The Fenchurch in the distance.

We bid Rachel and Jeremy goodbye in the lobby—they had plans to go and listen to a pianist in the Champagne Lounge—and took the elevator to our suite.

As soon as the large brass doors of the elevator slid shut, Shane dragged me up against his body. "I got harder with every step we took on the way back," he whispered onto my lips. "The thought of another night with you is driving me insane. I can't believe I got so lucky."

Wrapping my arms around his waist, I pulled him closer. He was right, he was hard. Very hard.

"You want to play a game?" I asked.

All the way back a thought had been nagging away at me. Shane's enjoyment of *Stolen and Seduced* had my mind racing with possibilities. There was something I needed to ask him while I had the courage of wine and felt so sublimely close to him.

"Only if it involves playing with you," he said, grinning.

"It does."

He cocked his head. "Go on."

I glanced at the lift numbers and the small upward arrow flashing. Could I really suggest it?

"Honey, tell me."

I swallowed and looked up into his face.

"You've got me curious," he said.

I dragged in a deep breath. I wasn't sure how he would take my suggestion but I hoped with all my heart it would appeal to him. "You know that book you read last night?"

"Yep."

"Well, it's one of my favorites and I wondered..." I paused. Would he think I was weirdly kinky or worse, completely freaky?

His voice lowered and his eyelids dropped slightly. "And you wondered if I fancied a little role-play?" His tone held a note of disbelief but also interest, and he'd certainly hit the nail on the head as to what I was suggesting.

My gaze snapped to his. "Yes."

"Oh, Ashley, I don't know if I'm ever going to be the same again after meeting you." He pulled me a little tighter. "You're a dream come true."

"Is that a yes?"

"Hell, yeah, the thought of you tied up like Eliza and your pleasure completely under my control is a massive turn-on. But are you sure? You only lost your virginity last night. I'd hate to scare you or do something you weren't comfortable with."

"Of course I'm sure or I wouldn't have suggested it. And as for having just lost my virginity, hell, I'm twenty-three, I figure I have a few years of sex to make up for."

The doors slid open and we stepped out into the fortunately deserted hallway. I would have died if anyone from Safe as Houses had heard that last sentence.

"Well, in that case, be prepared to be 'stolen and seduced', little lady," he whispered hotly into my ear. "But anything you really don't like, or if you want me to stop then just say," he paused, "Paddington Bear."

"Paddington Bear?"

"Yes, then I'll know that you mean it and you're not just getting into the role of Eliza and begging to be freed even when you don't want to be."

Paddington Bear. Okay.

I slid the keycard into our door and shoved it open. The room had been cleaned and smelled of polish. There was one dim lamp on in the living area.

"Go into the bathroom," Shane said, slipping out of his coat and throwing it over the back of the sofa. "And when you come out Hest will be waiting." He sat down and tugged off his wellington boots.

Heart fluttering, I quickly slipped out of my boots, nipped through the bedroom and into the en suite. With the door shut I leaned back against the wood. The bathrobes folded around my shoulders in a soft embrace. I felt giddy with anticipation, high with excitement. Oh my god! What had I asked for? And far from being shocked by my request, Shane had been up for it immediately. This was something I'd always dreamed of, being the heroine in one of my books—and now it was about to be realized.

Maybe I should have chosen a less dangerous scene. The one from *The Millionaire's Bride* would have been less wild and not at all kinky. But Shane hadn't read that one, he'd read, and enjoyed, *Stolen and Seduced*. Clearly fate had brought that scenario upon us and now there was nothing to do but enjoy.

Hastily, I brushed my teeth, staring all the time at my reflection. Once again there was something different about me, not just my rosy cheeks and windblown hair, but a hunger in my eyes, a longing, and a need that demanded to be satisfied buzzed between my legs and made my breasts heavy. Sex and getting naked with Shane was all I could think of.

I finished freshening up and slowly opened the door. The bedroom was in complete darkness. It was so black that when I clicked the bathroom light off I couldn't even see my hand in front of my face.

Taking a tentative step onto the carpet, my heart thudded. I struggled to catch my breath. The thrill of handing over this fantasy to Shane was off-the-Richter-scale sexy.

When will he grab me?

Will he be gentle and sweet or will he launch into the rough-and-tough role of Hest?

Walking farther into the room, slowly and hesitantly, I waited either to be captured or to bump my shins into furniture. I reached for something to feel my way around and blinked in the velvety blackness.

Suddenly a big palm clamped over my mouth and my head was pulled back into the solid muscle of a shoulder.

I yelped in shock but the sound was muffled.

"Keep quiet, Miss Winters, if you value your life!"

Something with an unnervingly metallic coolness pressed against my jugular, it slipped downward then around my neck, leaving a sharp trail of sensation.

My whole body froze, except for my heart rate, which rocketed. Surely Shane wouldn't use a knife for our game? It was what Hest had used but...

He must have sensed my real fear, for the sharpness lifted and I heard a double click. The "weapon" was a ball-point pen.

Phew!

The pen was back at my neck and his hot mouth by my ear. When he spoke, his voice was low and dangerous. It was easy to imagine in the darkness that it was Hest with a razor-sharp knife holding me tight.

"You've teased me for too long, Eliza. Made me want you until I was crazy with it and then you tossed me away. Do you really think you can do that with a man like me? Do you? Really?"

He moved his hand from my mouth and I slipped happily into role. "Hest, get off me. What the hell do you think you're doing?" I started to spin away but he clasped me to his body. His erection prodded at the small of my back and his arm became a tight band of granite around me. The pen flattened widthways over the lump in my throat.

"Oh, no, you don't, I have plans for you. Plans to make you mine, forever."

My excitement threatened to bubble over and my knees turned jel-ly-like. He even sounded like Hest and I swear his words were exactly the same as the book. Did he have a photographic memory or some-thing?

"You can't do this, my father will be out searching for me, no ex-pense will be spared. Hotel security will see us."

He laughed and lifted me as though I was no weight at all. As my feet left the floor, he began to stride forward, all the time speaking huskily into my ear. "No one will find you, Eliza, I've made sure we won't be seen, and besides, who would expect you to be held in the very place you were taken from? What kind of gangster would stay at The Plaza?"

I wriggled within his grip the way Eliza did in the story. Writhing and flailing. Fighting to be free. But it was no good, his hold was strong and firm and the more I tried to escape the tighter he held me. The pleasure of him increasing his grip urged me on with my squirming.

Suddenly, unexpectedly, he dropped me backward, fast. Luckily, I landed on the bed. Air whooshed from my lungs and immediately I scrabbled to the opposite side, enjoying the chase but knowing I wouldn't get away. And, of course, not wanting to get away.

"Oh, no, you don't." His full weight was over me, his hands roaming fast and wild, pulling and dragging at my clothes. "You can't escape, and soon you won't want to. Soon you'll come to realize only I can give you what you need, Eliza, and you'll admit it's me that you love, only me, for all of time."

Oh my, that was a bit too close to the truth. If I had to say those words, the lines between role-play and reality would blur. What if Shane *was* the man I was falling in love with for the first time? What if it *was* only going to be him for all eternity?

I didn't dwell on a truth that would overwhelm me if I admitted it. Instead I struggled and twisted as he tugged my sweater over my head and released my bra. Cool air breezed over my breasts, spiking my nipples so that they caught on the woolen material of his clothes as he pinned me down.

There was a soft whump as my sweater landed on the floor.

As we pushed and shoved at each other, our breaths quickened—mine rapid with excitement and exertion. Having him overpower me, physically dominate me so completely was thrilling and sexy. All of Eliza's thoughts and emotions tumbled with my own.

In a swift movement my arms were raised above my head. I knew what was coming but still it was a shock when something soft roped around them and snapped taut.

"Hest," I called, yanking at my shoulders. "What the—"

He silenced me with a kiss. A hot, hard, open-mouthed kiss that had me panting for breath. His lips were savage, he was as hungry for me as I was for him. His tongue plundered into my mouth, stealing every part of me and making me forget my own damn name. It was so different from his earlier reverent, careful kisses.

I loved it.

"Keep quiet," he snarled into my ear as he nibbled and licked across my cheek and on to my neck. "Keep quiet or I'll gag you."

I closed my mouth, stared into the darkness at where I knew he was and became totally still.

"You know what I am going to do, don't you, Eliza?"

"Please, no, let me go."

He chuckled in a mad, Dr. Evil kind of way. "Oh, but you don't really mean that, do you?"

"Yes, yes I do, let me go. Please, I want to go home."

He was silent for a long moment then whispered softly in my ear, "Do you need to say any words, honey?"

What? Does he think I am not having the time of my life? No way am I about to utter bloody Paddington Bear.

"No, no. Hest, just let me go. Let me go and I won't tell my father about this. I promise."

His voice was deep and gravelly when he spoke again, back in character. "Hah, I'm not scared of your father, and I'm not about to give up on you either, my love. I will tease you the way you have me, show you what you can have and then take it away."

He rose up and dragged at my jeans and knickers. I arched my spine and stiffened my legs, not wanting to make his job of removing my socks and fixing my ankles to the bedposts any easier.

But my struggle was futile and even in the blackness he attached me quickly and efficiently. Tight material wound around my lower legs. It was impossible to tug them free or close them even a little. My pussy was exposed and vulnerable, just as Eliza's had been. My arms were stretched high and taut, my back arched. An image of what I looked like filled my mind's eye—naked and bound to a four-poster bed, my hair wild and messed up and my breasts heaving with each frantic breath.

Thank goodness the lights were off. I must look such a sight. Shane's weight left the bed.

Brightness flooded the room.

Blinking rapidly, I gasped. There was no hiding now.

I looked down and spotted my stockings holding my ankles firm. Glancing up, I saw my new scarf wrapped tight around my wrists.

Shane stood at my side, half silhouetted by the light of the bedside lamp. He was still fully dressed. His hair was mussed and his chest rose quickly as he caught his breath. His gaze roamed my bound, exposed body as if he were a starving man looking at his favorite dinner.

If I could have moved I would have squirmed.

"Ah, my lovely Eliza, now you can have nothing unless I want you to have it." He dragged his sweater over his head in a quick, smooth movement. "You're mine to do with as I wish, and, sweetheart, I have lots I want to do with you."

He bent and latched his hot mouth over my right nipple. I pulled at my restraints as he nibbled gently and swirled his tongue deliciously. This was exactly what it must have been like for Eliza, there was no control. Hest decided the next thing to do to her. The helplessness, the vulnerability, it was so huge, so trusting—but because I *did* trust Shane it was also laced with a wonderful sweet security. He'd only made me feel good and I trusted him to continue making me feel that way.

"Please no," I murmured. "Hest, don't do this to me, to us. It's futile."

He ignored me as he explored my body with his fingertips, feeling right up to my poor trapped wrists, down the inside of my arms, my underarm and to the outer edge of my breasts. It tickled and I shivered at the light caress. Then he touched both my nipples. Tugged, pinched, rolled and tweaked until I writhed with pleasure and gasped for more.

He kissed lower, leaving my breasts wet and cooling and my nipples sharp points of bliss. When I realized what treat was coming my spine bowed like a lusty feline. But of course I *wasn't* coming. Hest hadn't let Eliza climax, even though she'd cried out in desperation. Begged in all manner of ways. That was what was really waiting for me. A ride *almost* to heaven.

Shane didn't need to spread my legs, they were already wide open. He swiftly settled between my thighs, parted my labia with his tongue and began to devour me as though my drenched pussy was the elixir of life itself.

"Eliza, you're so damn ready for me," he grunted, snuffling in deeper.

I bucked toward his face and cried out as he sucked my clit. Wet lapping sounds filled the room along with his groans of approval and my gasps of delight. He added his fingers to his tongue's ministrations and entered me high and fast.

"Oh god, Hest, please," I groaned, thrashing my head on the pillow and clamping my pussy around him. Nothing existed except the pleasure of being eaten out, worshipped, catapulted toward an almighty orgasm. I was almost there. My climax was a spring wound as tight as it could go. I was about to find my release—spectacularly.

Tearing open my eyes, I looked at his dark curls bobbing over my pussy and the tip of his nose buried in my pubic hair.

"Don't, don't stop."

He lifted his head.

Instantly, I realized my mistake and groaned in desperate disappointment. He wiped his forearm over his shiny mouth and glared down at me.

"You gonna admit you love me?" he growled.

"No, no, I can't because it's not true, but oh, please, let me, let me come."

"Tell me you love me." He pitched forward and dropped his elbows on either side of my head. His breath smelled of my pussy. "Say you love me, Eliza, and I will make you the happiest, most satisfied woman in the entire world. Say you'll be mine for all of time."

Twisting away, I whimpered in frustration. I'd been so near to orgasm. How could he? Okay, we were playing a game, but seriously?

"Damn it, woman," he muttered, standing.

There was a whiz of a zip and the rustle of material. Suddenly a thrill of cataclysmic proportions reeled through me as I remembered the next part of the book. The descriptions had been vivid and it was something I'd dreamed of doing for many years. And now, now with Shane Galloway, it was only moments away. I wasn't sure if I was going to be able to hold my desperately turned-on body together or become a puddle of wanton need strapped to a bed.

"You've got me so fucking hot for you," he snarled in a rasping voice as his jeans flew through the air and hit the opposite wall with a snap. His black boxer briefs followed. "You're going to have to sort me out and if you bite me, so help me god I will kill you, then myself."

His words were the exact ones written in the book.

Trembling in part delight, part nerves, I watched as he climbed over me and settled his knees on either side of my shoulders. His big body sank the mattress. The soft, black hairs on his thighs brushed the pale flesh on the outside of my upstretched arms and armpits.

He curved a hand around the nape of my neck and lifted my head to within inches of his jutting cock. I stared at it, marveling again at the size and the deep burgundy head, the slit that gaped and the neat rim of flesh flaring at the base of the glans.

He dropped his hips and the smooth tip nudged my lips. I glanced up and our eyes met, his were dark and filled with lust but there was something else there—concern, control, a need for reassurance.

He needn't have worried. More than anything I wanted to feel his cock slide over my tongue and touch the back of my throat. I'd read about it so many times and now I needed to feel that stretch in my jaw as I opened wide for his thick shaft. The thought of his flavor, of finally sampling the essence of a man, had my mouth watering. Saliva pooled in my cheeks and a dirty greed welled up inside me. It was a hunger so huge that I didn't know if it could ever be satisfied.

"Hest," I mumbled around his cock, begging him with my eyes. "Please."

His brow creased and the fingers around the back of my neck tightened.

"I want—"

He popped the head into my mouth, silencing my words. I gazed up at his face as my lips formed a wide "O". He was watching me carefully, as if checking I was coping, that I was okay.

In that moment I fell for him just a little bit more.

To ease his concern and show I welcomed the invasion, I poked the tip of my tongue into his slit. It was deep and firm but let me stretch it slightly. At the base I found a drip of salty fluid.

"Ah, fuck, you be careful doing that."

I didn't want to be careful. I wanted it all. I wanted to drive him as wild as he had just driven me with *his* mouth. My head was full of the story and the way Eliza had used her tongue to drive Hest crazy, torturing him with pleasure as a way of revenge for him teasing her.

Shane mumbled several guttural curse words and slid into my mouth farther. I strained my neck for more, his crude Hest-like language adding to my excitement. He fed another few inches of his shaft in and I drew the heated flesh to the back of my tongue, eagerly stretching my lips around his wide girth.

"Ah, Jesus." He was holding on to the back of the bed with his other hand, his position and the angle of my neck perfect for him to smooth in and out.

"When I've finished fucking your mouth, Eliza," he grunted as he set up a steady rhythm, "you'll say the words, the truth. If you don't I'm going to fuck you between your tits then your wet little pussy. I might even take your virginal arse if you still don't admit you love me the same way I love you. But you won't come, not once. Not until you say you'll be mine."

I rewarded his accurate memory of the book by sucking hard then scraping my teeth against his shaft. His body trembled and he hissed in a breath, his jaw clenching and his nostrils flaring. Then, as if control finally left him, he sank forward, driving his cock to the very back of my throat.

Squirming wildly, I gagged as his balls hit my chin, their baby-soft skin and silky hairs tickling.

Gulping for air, I finally overcame my gag and willingly surrendered to his cock.

He pulled back, watched me for a moment, again as if checking I was okay, then tipped his head to the ceiling and began to pump his hips, faster and faster, deeper and deeper.

My body was on fire, alive. I was close to orgasm. Shane using my helpless body, taking what he wanted was so sexy, the situation so erotic. It would take very little to tip me over the edge. If only I could squeeze my legs together. Just a small amount of pressure on my clit and I could finish what he'd started. I tried to move my hips, but of course I couldn't. I'd been stolen and strapped to a bed. Now I was being seduced in the most blissfully agonizing way imaginable.

"Heaven's above, get fucking ready for it," he grunted. His tone was harsh like Hest's and his words tight and scratchy as though the effort of speaking was too much.

Increasing the suction, I pulled at his crown with the muscles at the back of my throat. I wanted him to come, to unleash his desire as he reached maximum depth. I could barely catch my breath around his huge cock, but I didn't care.

He moaned loud and abandoned. The first drips of what was to come seeped onto my palate. He was pumping even faster now, his balls slapping against my chin, my nose burying in his pubic hair.

Pulling against my restraints, I bucked for more. I was drenched between my legs and my nipples sought any stimulation they could find on his thrusting body. Giving Shane this blowjob, drawing him to release had become my everything. The only thing that mattered.

"Ah, fuck, here it is," he cried, stilling at maximum depth. His cock swelled further, thickening and hardening. He gave one final, sudden thrust, then his seed poured from him, flooding the back of my mouth. I swallowed rapidly. I had no choice but to gulp down the copious fluid. It was that or drown in it. Each guzzle drew the head of his cock deeper and I sucked at the same time, as if urging it down my gullet.

"Oh my god, shit, that's it, yes, yes," he hissed, releasing the back of my neck.

Keeping my head held high, I reveled in the essence of him coating my tongue, rejoiced in the hardness of his jerking shaft and the depth I'd managed to take him.

"Jesus," he said, slipping from me.

I chased for his cock, not ready to give it up.

He flopped onto the bed next to me with his long limbs stretched out. "I'd planned on pulling out, but that swallowing you were doing made me lose it completely." He was panting hard, his words short and sharp.

I too was struggling for breath.

"That was fucking incredible, you sure you never done that before, honey?"

"Hest, you know I have, but only with you."

Huffing, he captured my chin in his hand. "In that case, Eliza, you are a naturally talented lady when it comes to giving pleasure with your mouth."

Mmm, I guess all that reading paid off.

Suddenly he stood from the bed and walked to the bathroom, shut the door and left me alone. My pulse thumped loud in my ears and my lungs ached as I continued to suck in the oxygen I'd been starved of. I licked my lips and swallowed, savoring the last splashes of his cum and the way my mouth felt stretched and used.

Chapter Seven

My pussy hummed as I lay spread-eagled waiting for Shane. I knew it was drenched too, no doubt marking the sheets. The air was cool on my exposed folds and I clenched my muscles, wishing for stimulation to take me over the edge of a climax.

But as I stared up at the tartan canopy, I was swamped with a sudden feeling of unfairness. Shane had come, yet I hadn't. I wanted to, desperately. No, make that *needed* to.

Okay we were role-playing, but did we have to stick to the plot line of *Stolen and Seduced* quite so accurately? What would one tiny orgasm matter?

The bathroom door opened and Shane sauntered out, shoving his hand through his hair and his semi-erect cock bobbing from his nest of pubes.

"Are you ready to say it?" he asked. His eyes were as black as night and his half-smile sinful.

Juddering in a breath, I shook my head.

He perched on the side of the bed and dipped his finger into my navel, then wound a path down to my pubic hair.

I gasped and bit on my bottom lip. "Are you sure you can't?" he asked.

"No, please, let me go."

I should just say it, really I should.

His wicked fingertip circled my clit, just the right amount of pressure. Perfect. And in that moment I cursed my insistence at finding an expert lover. This was one instance when it was going to backfire. Big-time.

Watching his movements, he upped the pace. I fluttered shut my eyes as my body fired straight back to the hovering state he'd left me in minutes before. Again I tried to close my legs, move my body. Though why I kept bothering I had no idea, it was futile, I was his hostage.

"Oh, Hest," I moaned. "Why are you doing this to me?"

"Because only I make you feel so alive, Eliza. Admit it, only I have ever made you feel this way."

"Yes, yes, only you." I could admit to that without it getting into any trouble.

The rotations around my needy nub continued. A climax was close. I tried to control my breathing, hold in my whimpers and gasps and keep my pelvis from rocking for more. I wouldn't make the same mistake again and let him know how close I was. Maybe I could even have a sneaky orgasm, once I'd let it take me it would be too late—he couldn't exactly steal it back.

And it was there, blooming wonderfully, his fingers teasing it out, building it up. My pussy clamped, preparing to lunge into ecstatic spasms. My clit was beginning to retract. I held my breath and awaited that state of bliss.

Suddenly he was gone. He'd stood from the bed and stopped touching me.

"Oh god, no," I cried, yanking furiously at my restraints. "That's not fair, please, I need this."

"So just say the words."

I meshed my lips together the way Eliza had done in the book. It was possibly the hardest thing I'd ever done in my life. Telling Shane I loved him would have been so easy to do. Telling him so he'd finish what he'd started would have been even easier. But I couldn't, because after that there would be no return. Saying it would give him my heart.

Oblivious to my dilemma, he smirked, walked to the desk and reached a bottle of water from the service tray. He folded his long frame into a chair and took a slug from the bottle. "You will," he said, hooking his ankle over his knee. "You will, eventually."

Sighing, I turned away, facing the opposite wall and studying the dark green fronds on the wallpaper. This was a stupid game. I just wanted to come. Why should I have to bare open my soul for an orgasm?

Shit, I'd been denied the pleasure of a man in my bed for so many years and now I had one, ready, willing and able, how had it come to this?

I must have slept, but for how long for I had no idea. When I opened my eyes the first thing I saw was Shane, still sitting in the chair. The water bottle was empty and his arms were crossed. He'd pulled on his boxer briefs.

Trying to move, I was quickly reminded of my bound, naked state.

He stood, opened another bottle of water and walked to the bed. Held it to my lips and cupped the nape of my neck the way he had when he'd slotted his cock into my mouth.

I took the water gratefully; my mouth tasted of sleep and semen.

"Are you ready to admit what you feel for me?" he asked in a low, murmuring voice.

"Hest," I pleaded. "You know it could never work between us, we're too different, what you're asking of me is pointless."

"No it isn't," he growled, "don't say that." His eyes darkened and I couldn't help but wonder what he'd been planning while I'd slept naked before him. A shiver of anticipation trickled across my flesh.

He placed the water down then shucked off his boxers to reveal his turgid, already sheathed cock. It bobbed up thick and angry and no sooner had my eyes widened at the sight of it than he was over me, prodding my entrance.

In one swift move he plunged in hard and fast, his way luckily well lubricated by my greedy pussy.

He set up a wild rhythm, pounding his hips in and out.

"Hest," I cried. "Oh god, Hest, why are you doing this?"

"Say it," he growled. "Say you love me, say you'll be mine for all of time."

I bit down on my lip, tasted blood. Oh, I was so in love with Shane Galloway. There was no point denying it to myself a moment longer. He'd stolen my heart as swiftly as he'd taken my virginity. It had been a fast, furious fall into lust and love and now I knew I would never, ever be the same again in so many ways.

His pubic bone was connecting wonderfully with my clit and I bucked for more, clamping my inner thighs around his legs as best I could and thrusting up to meet his savage thrusts. It was as if he just couldn't get deep enough. My pussy was straining to accommodate him at the same time it was delighting in the pain-pleasure stretching sensation.

Suddenly he withdrew and gripped my ankles. He fumbled for a moment with the stockings wrapped around the bedposts then released me.

Before I could do anything with my new semi-freedom I was flipped on to my stomach, my cheek squashed into the pillow and my breasts flattened beneath me. "What are you doing?" I asked on a gasp.

"You're one damn stubborn lady, but you met your match when you met me," he whispered harshly. "Talking to strangers in dark bars will only get you into trouble, as will teasing a man like me for six months straight."

Six months, oh, how I wish we'd had six months of this fun.

"You're going to take it from behind this time, Eliza, see if hitting your hot spot will persuade you to admit the truth in your heart."

Shane was well into the role of Hest now, even ad-libbing, and in a fleeting thought I wondered if he'd been reading the book again while I'd been sleeping.

I didn't have long to ponder because he wrapped his hands around my hips, settling his cock at my entrance. Bracing, for I could only imagine the intensity of what was coming, I balled my trapped hands into fists and stiffened my spine.

In one determined plunge he forged in, smoothing over what was definitely my G-spot as he tunneled on and on.

I called out in both pleasure and the overwhelming, deep, filling sensation. His cock was so long and thick and from this angle seemed to penetrate me higher than ever. And I could feel his bone-hard shaft and domed glans riding over my internal flesh wonderfully, connecting with a part of me that was crying out for pressure.

Leaning forward, he clamped a hand over my mouth and muffled my cry. "Quiet," he growled, "we don't want anyone raising the alarm and spoiling our fun, not when I have this room booked for the next two weeks if need be."

Milking his cock with my pussy, I whimpered, wishing I did have the luxury of staying in The Fenchurch with Shane for two weeks solid. I would surely die of pleasure if I could. What a sweet way to go.

He upped the pace, his hand still over my mouth. My orgasm was racing toward me again, it was so deep, building from a place I'd never had stimulated before. Briefly the urge to pass water consumed me and I groaned and wriggled. Shane just held me tighter, speeding up his already frantic thrusts, and I had no choice but to ride through it, capture the extreme pleasure again.

Suddenly it was there, within reach, one giant orgasm waiting to ravage every single fiber of my body.

He stilled, buried deep inside me and leaning tight into my back so his chest hair scratched at my shoulder blades. "Say it and I'll let you come. I know you like it like this, Eliza, only I truly understand what your horny little body needs. Only I can give you what you need for the rest of your life."

I opened my mouth behind his palm. The words sat on my tongue. It was no good, I had to tell him what I already knew. But saying Eliza's words would make them concrete and real. Telling Shane I loved him would give my heart permission to fling open its doors and welcome him in.

Plus, boy do I need to come!
"Yes," I managed. "Yes, yes, I do."

He lifted his hand and pressed his lips to my ear. "Say it," he groaned, pulling his cock out then thrusting back in, sliding wickedly over my supersensitive spot.

"Yes, yes, I love you so much."

"And you want me, you want to be mine." His voice was strained and his body a slab of solid concrete over me.

"Yes, I want to be yours, yes, please, let me come, I'm yours."

"Forever?"

"Yes, forever." He pulled out, lifting from my back then steaming in and out.

The orgasm that had been simmering for hours wreaked havoc on my body. "Ah, ah god, yes, yes," I shouted, turning my face into the pillow to muffle my subsequent squeals of delight, remembering that we did indeed have neighbors through the hotel wall.

His balls slapped against my labia as he pummeled into me, gripping my hipbones so tight I knew there'd be bruises. I didn't care. I'd handed myself over to him, heart and soul. Shane Galloway had just tunneled his way into my very core and would remain there forever. There was not a damn thing I could do about it.

My skin prickled, my breaths were hard to catch. On and on my pussy spasmed around his beautiful cock and I relished each tremor and convulsion he pulled from me. It was a wave of climaxes, cresting and falling, each one coming without warning. Each one a wonderful experience that started in my G-spot and spread out to the tips of my fingers and the ends of my toes.

"Ah, fuck," he cried.

As his shout echoed around the room, his cock pulsed within me, filling the condom with his pleasure. He continued to ride in and out, sending up decidedly unholy praises to the Lord as he did so.

His orgasm spiraled me into a final one of my own. I groaned long and abandoned into the pillow as satisfaction like nothing I'd ever known washed through me.

When our breathing and heart rates returned to normal, Shane carefully untied me then led me to the bathroom. He drew a deep bath full of sweetly scented bubbles and helped me step in.

"You okay, honey?" he asked, sitting naked on the edge of the bath and dipping a white washcloth into the water. It was the first time he'd spoken since our almighty climax.

"Yes."

"Did I hurt or scare you?"

I looked up at his anxious face. "You didn't, Hest did a bit."

He tugged at his bottom lip and frowned. "Oh god, I am so sorry. I got carried away, didn't I?"

I smiled. "No, not at all and don't be sorry, it was what I'd asked for and exactly the same as the book. I really did feel like Eliza."

"You did?" His eyebrows rose.

"Yes, you're a great actor, you're missing your vocation, you should consider being on the stage."

He chuckled, rubbing a milky white bar of soap onto the washcloth.

"You were spot on with the lines," I said.

"I figured if that's your favorite book you'd know it pretty well." Placing the soap in the dish, he motioned for me to tip forward slightly. "I didn't want to screw it up for you."

"You didn't, it was fun." I paused. "More than fun, it was amazing, though I was very frustrated on more than one occasion."

He carefully rubbed the lathered washcloth over my back, dipping around my neck and into my armpits. My shoulders ached slightly and the sensation was soothing.

"That was the idea, remember? Until you said those words, there was no orgasm for you."

Those words were indelibly printed on my mind. *I love you so much, I want to be yours, forever.* When Margaret Rider wrote them, I bet she never imagined they'd play such a pivotal role in someone's real life. Because here I sat, little Ashley Jones, in a luxury hotel suite with the man of my dreams, and I'd just told him that I loved him and wanted to be with him forever.

Of course he hadn't said them back.

Shutting my eyes, I hugged my knees and reveled in Shane's soft, caring touch. How the hell had I gotten into this situation?

Oh yes—Dawn!

By the time Shane had also bathed it was getting late and we were hungry again. I rang for sandwiches and a pot of tea while he put on the fire and shut the curtains in the living area. He found a romantic comedy just starting on TV and when I sat next to him on the sofa, he reached over and pulled me close.

"I had fun this afternoon too, you know," he said, putting his feet up onto the coffee table and crossing his ankles.

"That was the idea." I folded my legs up under my robe.

"And you really were, are very good at...you know..."

I looked up at his handsome face. His stubble was getting denser with each passing hour. I moved a damp lock of his hair away from his eye. "At what?"

"At..." He hesitated.

"At sucking your cock."

He laughed. "Yes, Ashley, you were really very good at sucking my cock."

I grinned.

"And you picked up all your skills from reading erotic romance?"

"Yes, I guess so, if you can call them skills."

"Oh yes, they're skills, all right, because without a doubt you're the sexiest, most liberated, most responsive woman I've ever been with. And to think only yesterday I had the honor of taking your virginity." He lowered his voice. "Someone in the heavens was definitely shining down on me when you walked into that restaurant, because you are, by far, the best thing that's happened to me all year."

My pesky heart beat a little harder for him but I resisted telling him he was the best thing that had happened to me *ever*.

"And I can't wait to read some more of your raunchy books. Perhaps you could suggest some titles and I'll read them so when I come to London we can play more games." He brushed his lips to mine. "Would you like that?"

"Sounds like a great idea." My mind spun. Oh my, what to choose? *The Barmaid's Brew* had some steaming hot scenes but could I cope with a whip? What would Shane think if I suggested trying? Perhaps if we were out on the town I could steal a moment from *A Mistress for Midnight* and perform oral sex on him in a deserted tube train the way Georgina did to Raif. That would of course depend on us finding a deserted tube train.

A sudden rap at the door shook me from my erotic thoughts. I jumped up and answered it. A suited bellboy wheeled in a trolley laden with egg and cress sandwiches, tuna and cucumber rolls and colorful fondant fancies. There was also an enormous pot of tea, and rose-patterned china.

Shane tipped him and we settled down to eat our supper on the sofa.

"So, er, when do you think you might visit London?" I asked, staring at the movie. It starred Jennifer Aniston but I couldn't recall the name of it.

"As soon as I can if it's okay with you."

"Of course, just let me know." Biting into a sandwich, I tried not to think about how it would feel saying goodbye to him in the morning. Knowing it would be hours, days, possibly weeks before we were together again. I didn't know how I would be able to breathe without him, let alone function.

"I'm spending Christmas with my sister," he said, "she's had a rough time too, split with her guy of eight years. And since it is only the second Christmas since we lost our parents, we kind of promised each other to hang out."

"That's nice, to spend it together that is."

"And you?"

"With my parents, they live in Surrey."

He nodded and looked thoughtful for a moment. "But then I'm not doing much for New Year, maybe I could travel down if you'll be back in the city by then."

Reaching for the teapot, I poured us both a cup. "Yes, I'll be home by then."

"Great." He added two big spoonfuls of sugar to his tea. "We could go to Trafalgar Square and jump in the fountains at the stroke of midnight." Sipping his steaming drink, he looked over the brim of his cup at me. "And then go back to your place. Hopefully you'll have found me a novel to read by then that you want to mess around with."

I grinned. It sounded like a perfect plan and as he said it a delicious scene from *Swashbuckling on the High Seas* came to me. Captain Hawkeye was rather fond of spanking; something told me Shane would get quite into that role if I put it to him.

"But I'll call you on Christmas Day," he said. "You know, say hi, see how it's going with your parents and get a tally on how many mince pies you've eaten compared to me."

I giggled. "Yes, I'll look forward to it."

After we finished eating and the movie had come to an end, Shane fulfilled his and my desire to make love on the sofa.

Without saying a word, he tucked me beneath him, looked deep into my eyes and entered me. Slowly but surely he brought us both to a mind-altering climax by doing nothing more than rocking his sinfully talented hips.

I clung to him afterward, panting. Heat from the fire competed with the heat pouring from our bodies, and my pussy gripped and released his cock for what felt like an eternity.

His masculine smell invaded every breath I took, his taste filled my mouth and his body seemed to touch every inch of mine, inside and out. I was lost to him, nothing and no one else existed.

My life would never be the same again.

Eventually he smoothed the hair back from my damp forehead and kissed me, softly, gently, before exploring my neck, behind my ear and down to my shoulder. I fluttered my eyes shut and felt the sweet envelope of sleep engulf me. It took me to a wondrous place of love and passion, peace and contentment.

A place that consisted of only Shane and me.

Chapter Eight

I pulled into the parking lot of Safe as Houses and yanked on the handbrake, knowing as I performed the sharp gesture that I shouldn't be so rough. My foul mood wasn't my little VW's fault and this was, after all, its first trip out this year.

Before reaching for my purse, I stretched to look at my eyes in the rearview mirror. Yep, as bad as I suspected. Why Radio One still thought it was okay to play Wham's *Last Christmas* on the fourth of January I had no idea. The damn thing had set me off all over again, just when I'd brought my emotions under control ready to face everyone.

After searching for the handkerchief that was permanently shoved up my sleeve these days, I set about blowing and powdering my nose and applying a slick of clear gloss to my lips. I then added two drops of Bright Eyes into each of my lower lids. Marvelous stuff. By the time I got up to the office, as long as nothing else set me off, I wouldn't look as though I'd sobbed all the way to work.

Stepping onto the now snow-free tarmac, I straightened the outfit I'd bought on my way back from The Fenchurch. Still high on my own personal drug, which was of course Shane, I'd stopped at a designer retail outlet and blown my entire bonus on snazzy new clothes. They were all Dawn style and each look had been completed with killer shoes, funky costume jewelry and break-the-bank handbags. Who cared, I'd been happy, in love, I'd needed this stuff for all the hot dates I had in my future.

My parents had been very complimentary of the "new me" on Christmas Day. They'd liked my skinny jeans and green sweater teamed with Ugg boots and a faux-fur-lined jacket. Mum had especially gushed over the chunky bracelet and green hoop earrings I'd added. It hadn't taken her long to guess there was a man in my life. She made quick work of cornering me in the kitchen under the pretense of needing help with the vegetables.

But once I started talking about Shane and how wonderful he was I couldn't stop, just saying his name and picturing his face made me smile and caused my heart to swell. Mum didn't seem to mind and grinned and nodded and asked all the right questions. Naturally, I refrained from adding any details of how skilled he was in the bedroom or how much he'd enjoyed acting out a racy scene from my favorite book.

As the day went on I started to clock watch. He'd said he'd call to compare mince pie consumption. Dinner was eaten and cleared away, the Queen made her speech and, as he did each year on Christmas afternoon, James Bond saved the world. Afterward, helping Dad make the turkey sandwiches for supper, I could feel my mood sinking.

Finally my cell rang. Late. After ten at night. "Ashley?"

"Shane," my voice bubbled with relief.

"Happy Christmas."

"You too, have you had a nice day with your sister?"

"Yes, fine, quiet. You?"

"Lovely. Mum did a great spread of food, far too much for the three of us."

There was a pause.

"Sounds nice," he said.

Another pause.

"Did you watch James Bond?" I asked. Something was wrong. I could tell. His voice was distant, preoccupied. "Shane, are you okay?"

"Um, yep, fine, has the snow gone there?"

"Yes, pretty much, a few sprinkles on high ground."

We chatted for a few minutes but he seemed distracted. Eventually I asked again, "Are you sure everything is okay?"

"Yes, honey, it's fine, but listen I can't really chat now, got lots on, with, er, my sister and that, but I'll catch up with you soon, okay?"

"Oh, all right then."

"Bye, Ashley, take care."

"Yes, you too, see you."

The line went dead.

The week passed between Christmas and New Year without another word from him and it was as though my heart had died too.

Finally, on the stroke of midnight on New Year's Eve, I'd received a text.

Happy New Year. Sorry I'm not there, see you soon. Shane xxx

Well, if he couldn't be bothered to ring and tell me *why* he wasn't here or *when* he intended to see me, then I certainly didn't want to respond to a crappy text message. Not when he'd been supposed to actually, physically be with me on New Year's Eve.

So apart from one brief, stilted conversation and one text message we'd had no contact since saying goodbye at The Fenchurch. He'd kissed me through the open window of my car and waved me off. I'd nearly hit a tree as I'd watched him in my rearview mirror climbing into his Golf, feasting on every last moment of seeing him.

Sighing, I pushed open the front door to Safe as Houses and nodded an overbright hello to Samantha the receptionist. Why I was thinking of all this now I had no idea. I'd spent days moping around my flat, crying, eating chocolate and trying desperately to lose myself in fiction.

How could he behave like this? How could he have said the things he did if he'd never wanted more than a bit of fun while we were snowed in? I was a big girl. I could have handled the truth. But acting as though it was going to be more, as though I meant something to him, was just plain cruel.

The thing was, I knew in my heart of hearts that Shane wasn't a cruel man. The only explanation was that he'd got caught up in the moment and it had made him say things he didn't really feel. So with that in mind, I'd faced the truth. To him, I was a two-night stand with a bit of kinky fun thrown in. A notch on his bedpost after going through a post-divorce sex drought. I tried to find comfort in the fact that I'd had a great time and my damn virginity had been well and truly gotten rid of.

But the way it had ended between us made the memories bitter-sweet. And the image of his face and the scent of his skin, instead of fading, each day just intensified, ripping open the hole in my heart afresh every morning when I awoke and remembered he was never going to be part of my life, and that all he'd left me with was a whole vat of longing.

I climbed the flight of stairs to my office. At least Dawn wasn't going to be there today. She'd texted to say she'd had a sudden opportunity to go skiing for New Year so wouldn't be in until the eighth. That suited me. I would tell her most of what happened, but on this first day back I was too raw and I really didn't want to cry at work. I'd made a pact with myself not to. I'd get my head down, go to whatever meetings I was called to and work through my customer list. If I could get through the day without one tear in public, then I'd reward myself with a new ebook tonight. But not a contemporary, something paranormal, preferably where the hero gets hunted down and bitten, hard. Henrietta Dowling's new title *Savaged by Virgins* sprang to mind and I made a mental note to add it to my cart.

Dumping my new handbag on my desk, I whizzed my laptop to life. Stepping to the window did nothing to improve my mood. The January sky lay gray over the London rooftops, the sun barely visible through the blanket of mist.

"Hey, Ashley, Happy New Year."

I turned to see Gareth standing in the doorway to my office. "Happy New Year to you too," I said.

"Love the new skirt." He grinned, dropping his gaze down my white silk blouse to the tight black pencil skirt I was wearing, then on to my sheer stockings and patent heels.

"Thanks."

His smile broadened. "Did you hear about Derek retiring?"

"Yes, I was at The Fenchurch when it was announced." I tensed and willed my traitorous body not to react to the name of the hotel where I'd given my heart away.

"Oh yeah, 'course you were. Quite a shock though, thought the old guy would hang around for a bit longer yet."

"Well, he's got lots he wants to do with Janice, I think he'll be kept very busy."

"He's coming in at ten though, to announce who'll be taking over from him." Gareth rubbed his hands together.

"You fancy your chances?" I asked, bending over and tapping in my password.

He shrugged. "Why not, stranger things have happened."

I nodded. "Yes, well, good luck if that's what you want."

He tipped his head. "Don't you? You've been here for five years."

"No, it's not what I want at all." There was only one thing, one person I wanted and that was never going to happen, not now.

Pulling in a deep breath, I forced myself to smile, praying that Gareth wouldn't hang around for too much longer. I needed to be alone, it was the best thing for me in my current state.

"Well, if I do get it, Ashley, I'm going out celebrating and you," he paused and a devilish grin tipped his mouth, "should be prepared to come with me for a wild night at Dover Street Bar."

He was hopeful and enthusiastic, I could give him that. So I muttered something noncommittal and pretended to be engrossed in my emails. Thankfully, he wandered away, albeit humming a damn Christmas tune.

I came across an email from Rachel and clicked it open.

Hi Ashley,

I just wanted to say what a wonderful time I had at The Three Horseshoes that snowy, stolen afternoon. The food and the pub were perfect but it was the company that made it really special.

I hope you'll stay in touch as a friend and not just a work colleague and I hope all goes well between you and Shane. You really are a match made in heaven and it was clear how happy you made each other that day.

Rachel x

I stabbed my finger at the keyboard and hit delete.

Match made in heaven!

There was never a worse statement written, because right now I felt as if I'd been dragged to hell—a deep, burning, nasty pit of hell that I could see no way out of.

Quickly I opened a dull email about insurance premiums and read the details, willing my eyes not to fill. It was sweet of Rachel, but how could I be her friend when she would only remind me of what I'd had and then lost?

With effort I pushed Rachel's words from my mind. I could revisit them later in the privacy of my flat where crying or throwing something at the wall wouldn't be an issue.

In a flurry of activity, I read through a dozen emails and replied to them all.

"You ready?"

I glanced up.

Gareth was at my door again, pointing at his watch. "For the ten o'clock announcement," he said, widening his eyes as if I was being completely daft not to remember.

"Oh, of course, yes." I stood quickly and grabbed my file. I had a couple of things to go through with Derek if he was going to be in the office one last time.

We took the elevator to the fourth floor, Gareth chatting about a new phone he'd picked up in the sales. It was an enormous effort in my miserable condition to mumble appropriate upbeat responses.

Stepping out of the elevator, I had a sudden panic as I remembered Shane saying he'd bumped into Derek when he'd been emptying the condom machine.

Oh god, Derek knows we slept together.

How would I face him? My cheeks flushed and my clothes suddenly felt too tight. Gareth was raving on about some new app while I wanted the floor to swallow me up.

We approached the office and I knew I had no choice, I had to go and sit at that long oval desk and listen as the next branch manager was announced, regardless of what my old boss knew of my sex life.

I swallowed tightly and braced my spine. I was twenty-three, so what if I'd had sex with a gorgeous guy? That's what twenty-three-year-olds did. Tilting my chin, I tried to feel brave. Who was I kidding, brave had never been my forte.

Gareth politely held open the large wooden door but frowned as I brushed past him. "You okay? You look a bit pale."

"Er, yes, fine." Nausea clenched my guts. I knew without looking in a mirror there was no blood in my face. This was going to be excruciating. A bit like confessing to my dad that I'd had wild, wanton sex with a man I barely knew.

Gareth, obviously not convinced of my state of health, stepped ahead and pulled out my chair. He still looked worried. As I sat down he tucked it in for me. I placed my folder on the table and looked around the room.

My breath caught in my throat, the nausea in my stomach swirled. If I'd been pale before, now I felt positively ghostly. For there, at the top of the table, in front of the whiteboard, sat not only Derek, but also Shane-bloody-Galloway.

As my heart rate rocketed I heard my own gasp. Quickly I bit down on my bottom lip.

He wore a pristine charcoal suit, a pale-blue shirt and a navy-and-white-striped tie. His hair was neat, it had been trimmed, and he was clean shaven. Well, almost. He still sported a little dark stubble over his top lip and around his chin.

His hands were resting on the table, fingers splayed, and his black-er-than-black gaze was directed, unblinking, at me.

"Coffee?" Gareth asked, his shoulder touching mine as he poured without waiting for an answer.

"Er, yes," I managed, though it felt as if my mouth and throat were full of cotton wool.

What the hell is Shane doing here?

I tore my gaze from his. How was I supposed to hold it together when he was sitting there looking like every one of my fantasies and desires rolled into one hot specimen of a man?

Bastard.

Derek started talking about his retirement plans. Gareth added a heaped spoon of sugar to my coffee and stirred. Out of the corner of my eye, I saw Shane add two to his. I couldn't look at him directly. I feared my heart wouldn't hold out. He was so painfully gorgeous and no longer mine to touch and hold.

I took a sip of coffee as Gareth and Derek had a conversation about marketing strategy that went over my head. My eyes actually physically stung, my chest ached. I glanced up. Shane was still staring at me, his eyebrows pulled low as he spun a ball-point pen around his fingers.

I crossed my legs beneath the table. My knee jolted into Gareth's. He paused in what he was saying and glanced at me.

"Sorry," I mouthed. I had to get out of there. I was going to faint or vomit or run over and poke Shane's damn silver pen up his nose, up his ass or anywhere else I could shove it.

Oh god, the pen.

The memory of him holding a pen like that one at my throat overwhelmed me. I could still hear him whispering dirty, hot words into my ear as he captured me in the darkness. For a second I was back there, in the hotel room, his arms tight around me, his breaths hard and fast, as excited as I was about our game. I shut my eyes but that only served to remind me of the sudden toss onto the bed and the subsequent tying up of my limbs. I squirmed on my chair, my pussy clenching at the memory of the torment he'd expertly put me through. It had been so sexy, so frustrating, and so completely wild when we'd finally come together. And the words, the words I'd shouted just before I came.

I love you so much. I want to be your....forever...please, let me come.

Those damn words were still the truth, as I'd known they would be even before I'd uttered them.

"Ashley, I'm sure that will be fine with you, won't it?" Derek asked.

"I, um, what?" Drawn from my erotic memories, I refocused on the end of the table. Derek was smiling at me expectantly.

"To help Shane, as he settles in."

"But..." I glanced at Gareth, hoping for help.

He raised his eyebrows at me. "But I—"

"Ashley, Shane will need all the information you have on prospective customers and past clients, particularly industry. I'd be grateful if you'd go through it with him as soon as possible."

"I don't understand."

Derek smiled kindly then stood, leaning his knuckles on the table in front of him and beaming around the room. His jowls wobbled and his face was red. He looked as though he was about to burst.

"I should probably explain to everyone more clearly then," he said. "Shane Galloway is..." he paused and stretched his smile even wider, "is your new branch manager, and I hope you'll all join me in welcoming him."

Gareth muttered something under his breath, but I didn't catch it because at that moment it was as if all the blood in my body had raced to my ears. I could hear my pulse pounding, thumping through every vein and artery in my head.

Shane was my new boss.

Oh, fuck.

Now I'd never be able to get him out of my heart. Never be able to get over him. Every day he'd be there, looking all drop-dead, heart-stoppingly gorgeous. No doubt he'd soon start dating the fabulously glamorous Dawn. No man could resist her, and I'd have to watch them fawn over each other all day every day.

As several people got up to shake Shane's hand and congratulate him I mentally went through my contract. Was it a week or a month notice I had to give? I couldn't be sure. But either way it shouldn't take long to find another job. I had a good working record and Derek would give me a decent reference.

I grabbed my coffee and gulped. As I put it back down a little splashed over the side. Using the handkerchief from my sleeve, I mopped up the spillage.

"Shit, what does he have that I don't?" Gareth muttered under his breath.

Opening my mouth, I hesitated. What could I say? Shane was doing a marketing degree, he had a photographic memory and fabulous acting skills. Not to mention a beautiful cock that tasted divine and fitted in my mouth and pussy perfectly. Or maybe that he knew how to manipulate the end of a shower attachment in a way that was truly sinful. I didn't think Gareth wanted to hear any of those facts. I shut my mouth again.

"So," Derek said, clamping a beefy arm around Shane's shoulders. "I know I said I didn't want a fuss, but I'm buying drinks tonight at The Cow and Slipper for all my wonderful team, so see you there about eight." He squeezed Shane's shoulder. "You too, young man, you too."

I scraped back my chair and stood. Gareth had already left the room. He'd be pissed about Shane coming in and taking the top spot, but he'd get over it. What choice did he have? The problem was *I* wouldn't get over it. Shane was here but he wasn't mine. Last time I'd seen him we'd kissed, made love, laughed, talked of the future. No, I had no choice. My time at Safe as Houses had come to an abrupt end.

Grabbing my folder, I slipped from the room without another glance at Shane. I took the stairs instead of the elevator. I couldn't bear the thought of making polite small talk with anyone.

Once back in my office I dropped my head in my hands and willed myself not to cry. How could this have happened? If only Dawn hadn't played that stupid trick of switching my dress, I wouldn't be in this position now. I'd have a hunky new boss, sure, but I wouldn't have slept with him, I wouldn't have had my heart broken by him. "Damn you to hell, Dawn," I muttered.

"Ashley."

I lifted my head at the sound of Derek's deep voice

"Are you okay, poppet?" he asked, stepping into my office.

I nodded and gulped down a sob. I would not cry.

"I know it's a shock having a new boss," he said. "Particularly Shane Galloway."

"It makes no difference who it is, I'm just going to miss it being you." I beat down a tremble in my voice. I wasn't sure how successful I'd been when his face twisted sympathetically.

"That's sweet of you to say, but I, er...know you like Shane." He shifted from foot to foot and looked at the floor.

"Yes, yes, absolutely." I nodded a bit too briskly. "I'm sure he'll be a great addition to the Chelsea branch."

He narrowed his eyes at me. "Mmm, are you upset about something else?"

"No, no, of course not."

"You had no interest in the position, did you?"

"Oh, gosh no, I've told you lots of times, I'm very happy with what I'm doing, I like chatting to the customers and I'm not really qualified for the top spot anyway."

He smiled, as if relieved. "Good, because I did tell Shane when he accepted the job on Christmas Eve to keep it a secret that he was being made branch manager. I made him promise not to tell a soul. I know it will have put a few noses out of joint, him stepping in, and I needed him to have the element of surprise to cope with that, which I'm sure he will, admirably."

"When did you say you offered him the job?"

"On Christmas Eve. He took less than an hour to decide and call me back."

"Oh." At least he hadn't known that he was going to be my new boss when we'd been together at The Fenchurch. I turned to my computer and brought up my inbox. It was still jammed with flagged messages.

Derek sighed. "Well, as long as you're all right, I'll leave you to it. I can see you're very busy. But will you come along tonight to The Cow and Slipper for a drink?"

"Yes, yes, of course, see you later." No way was I going. I, for one, wasn't some kind of masochist when it came to my heart and soul.

He left the room and I was alone once more. I prayed it would stay that way. That Gareth wouldn't come blundering in gassing off about the position he should have had. I couldn't cope.

In fact, sod it, I'd just go home. Today needed wiping out. I gathered my purse and coat. Flicked off my laptop and formed a lie about a migraine to tell anyone I met on the way to my car.

My desk phone trilled to life. I stared at it. Sighed. Picked it up.

"Ashley, it's me."

My jaw clenched so tight I feared for my teeth. "What do you want, Shane?"

"I need you to come up to my office, now."

"I can't."

He hesitated. "Why not?"

"I'm going home."

"You are, why?"

"I have a terrible headache. A migraine in fact."

"Do you want me to drive you?"

Is the man nuts? Get in a car with him!

"No, I can drive myself."

"Well, do you have any medication?"

"Er, yes, I think so, probably something in the cabinet."

The line was quiet.

"Ashley—"

"Shane, I have to go."

"Come up to my office first, I need to speak to you."

My stomach was tying itself in knots and I really *was* getting a headache now. "I don't know what you can possibly have to say to me. I'll forward all the information you need tomorrow, from home if I'm still unwell. My going won't affect you at all."

"Ashley, come to my office."

I stared out the window—a crow squawked from the opposite rooftop and flapped its wings.

"Ashley, I'm not asking," his said, his voice deepening "I'm telling."

I sucked in a breath. "Seriously?"

"Yes, seriously, I'm your boss, now get up here this instant, I want to speak to you."

I slammed down the phone so hard I hurt my hand.

Not asking, telling! Who the hell does he think he is?

Marching from the room, I headed for the elevator and rode to the fifth floor. I nodded a curt hello to head secretary Hilda, then found myself standing outside the heavy oak door of what was once Derek's office and was now my ex-lover's.

Straightening out my thin blouse, I tossed my hair over my shoulders, pulled in a deep, fortifying breath and knocked. The sooner this was over with the better.

"Come in."

I stepped into the large wood-paneled room. Shane stood on the other side of a shiny mahogany desk. It was neat and ordered, unlike the way Derek always had it.

"Close the door," he said.

I did as he asked then clasped my hands together, wishing they weren't trembling and my breaths weren't so rapid. Wishing for all the world that he wasn't such a truly beautiful man.

"Would you like a drink, a glass of water?" he asked.

I shook my head.

He walked toward me, his pace fast and his strides long. Instinctively I took a step back. Shane had hurt me more than anyone else ever had. I couldn't cope with him coming near me again. His smell and the heat of his body would only serve to increase my agony.

"Ashley?" He stopped in his tracks. Distress flashed in his eyes.

I shook my head and tightened my lips. "Don't come near me."

"But...but I can explain."

"I don't think so."

He sighed and rubbed his forehead. "Please, sit down, let me try."

"I'd rather stand because I'm not staying long. I want to go home." I walked to a long, low windowsill. Looking down, I realized just how high this office was—there were only rooftops, chimneys and air-conditioning units for neighbors. No windows to look in on him.

He followed me and I turned with a frown.

"Ashley it's not what you think."

"I might have been a virgin when we met, Shane, but I'm not stupid."

"I know you're not—"

"So nothing you can say can make it better. It must have been awkward for you to be offered this position after you'd made me another notch on your bedpost." I jabbed my hands onto my hips. "But did it even go through your mind how difficult it would be for *me* to work with *you*?" My voice twisted with sarcasm. "Well, of course, that is, if you could even remember my name."

He lifted his eyebrows, creating crinkles in his forehead.

"No, I don't suppose you cared did you, Shane? You were climbing the career ladder. Just look at this fabulous office and all the millions of pounds worth of contracts you're responsible for now. What did it matter if you'd slept with the office mouse on her one weekend of bravery?"

"Ashley, I—"

"But don't you worry, because I'm leaving. In fact you can take this conversation as my notice." I stabbed his tie with my index finger. "I quit."

His mouth hung open.

"I...quit." I punctuated each word with another jab of my finger. "Get it? I'm finished here, as of now." I spun and stalked to the office door. "Goodbye, forever."

"Ashley, for god's sake." He wrapped his hand around my upper arm and twisted me to face him. "Will you just bloody listen?"

I gasped and drew in his sumptuous light aftershave. "Get off me."

"Not until you hear me out."

"You don't need to explain. You wanted sex, I was there. But now that we're back in the real world I'm of no interest to you."

He grabbed my other upper arm and dragged me up against his body. My breasts pressed against his lapels and I could make out the solid muscle beneath. I shivered at the sudden erotic memory of our bodies pressed together hot and naked and sweaty.

"No interest," he snarled, his black eyes boring into mine.

"Yes, no interest. You hardly spoke to me on Christmas Day and then you didn't come at New Year, just sent me a lousy text. Well, I got the message loud and clear. Not interested."

"I told you I can explain, but we'll start with this so you hear what *I'm* saying loud and clear."

He released my left arm, slid his hand down my spine to the hollow of my back and forced my pelvis into his.

I sucked in a breath. Beneath his smart suit pants his steely cock strained forward and pressed into my mound.

"I *am* interested," he said, his hot breath washing on to my cheek. "More than bloody interested. I've been hard ever since I got in the car yesterday and made the journey down the M1 to start this new job, and do you want to know the main damn reason I took it?"

I gulped.

"Because, Ashley, *you're* here."

Balling my fists, I pressed them onto his shoulders. "Don't say things that aren't true."

"It is true." His face crumpled, as if he was in pain. "I'm so sorry. I didn't know what to do. Derek called me on Christmas Eve and offered me the position on behalf of Ray Burgess. We were on the phone for hours talking through relocation, what it meant for me career-wise and what support structure would be in place."

My legs felt weak, my stomach churned.

"But he told me in no uncertain terms that it had to be kept a secret. I wasn't to tell anyone, least of all anyone here, at this branch. If I did, and word got out, the promotion would be retracted."

"But you could have told me." My eyes were filling with tears, I could feel them forming on my lower lids.

"Ah, honey, don't you see? They were testing me." He gave a stiff shrug. "How could I fail that first test? The competition was tough for the job and I hadn't even officially applied. It was going to ruffle feathers and they knew it." He relaxed his tight hold but kept me wrapped in his arms. "On Christmas Day I'd put off ringing you because I knew you'd hear excitement in my voice. I wanted so badly to tell you but I couldn't."

I shook my head. "You were positively miserable, not to mention abrupt."

"I'm so sorry, please forgive me."

Forgive him?

He'd put my emotions through a spin dryer. I no longer knew which way was up and which way was down. How could I forgive him?

"Ashley, you have to understand."

A tear broke its banks and trickled down my cheek. I cursed and twisted from his embrace, hunting out my now ragged, coffee-stained handkerchief.

"I didn't mean to hurt you," he said. "But I had no choice but to keep quiet. And I knew if I spent New Year with you, after a couple of drinks and well, you being you, I would have told you everything. I thought it best to just stay away."

I spun to him, sniffing miserably as I did so. "Do you know what I've been through? To think that you mean something to someone and then find out it's all a load of rubbish."

"Yes, yes, I do know what that's like. It's a pile of shit."

Folding my arms, I suddenly felt mean. Mandy had made him feel like that. And they'd been married. That had been so much more than a two-night stand.

"But perhaps we can put all that behind us now. Start anew." He reached for me again and my traitorous body allowed him to tug me close. I couldn't help it, he was irresistible.

"Honey," he whispered, tucking a strand of hair behind my ear. "We're so good together. Remember all the fun we had, how comfortable we were in one another's company? I've never felt like that before, ever. We just clicked."

Oh, he was good all right. He so nearly had me again.

"Shane," I murmured on a juddering breath. "It hurt so much. I don't know if I can just forget it."

His eyes narrowed and I saw my pain reflected in them. "I'm not asking you to forget it, just forgive me and I'll do everything in my power to make it up to you." His soft lips brushed mine. "I'll show you that you need never doubt me again."

"But how will 'this' work?"

He grinned suddenly. "Well, it's going to be a damn sight easier than when I was living in Huddersfield."

"True."

"Because then I thought I was going to have to spend half my wages on fuel each weekend coming down to London."

"You would have done that?"

"Of course."

Okay, he has me.

I reached up and kissed him. Pressed the whole length of my body into my new boss and delved my tongue into his mouth.

Eagerly he returned my kiss, pulling me tight and almost lifting me off the floor so just the tips of my toes pressed into the carpet.

"Oh, Ashley," he murmured. "I'm not letting you go again. Watching you drive away from The Fenchurch was one of the hardest things I've ever done."

"So was driving away." I kissed across his cheek, his stubble scratching my chin and lips.

"So don't ever leave again. This is it, me and you."

"Yes, me and you." I felt my heart would burst with joy. After being shattered into a million tiny pieces suddenly it was back together again. Shane made me feel this way, only Shane. I'd waited so long for him to come into my life. I'd lost him and now he was back. I wasn't letting go.

He spun me so my bum hit the desk. I shuffled up onto it, dragged up my skirt and wrapped my legs around his thighs.

"Ah, fuck, we can't do this here," he groaned, looking down at me with lust-filled eyes and pushing my skirt higher still.

"No, no, we can't," I said, tilting my pelvis so the gusset of my panties pressed on his cock through his pants. "Absolutely not."

"But we do have lost time to make up for, New Year's Eve."

"Yes, lost time." I shoved my fingers through his hair. "New Year's Eve I'd planned an elaborate reenactment from *A Mistress for Midnight*."

"Oh god," he whispered. "Not the deserted train scene?"

I pulled back and stared at his face. I really hadn't seen that coming.

He grinned, that cheeky, slightly wonky grin I adored. "In the last two weeks I've read every Margaret Rider book there is because you, naughty lady, have me well and truly hooked."

Licking my lips, I smiled back at him. "So you fancied me sucking your cock on the Underground?"

His jaw visibly slackened. "Oh god, yes. You do that like no one else.

"Want me to do it now?"

"Shit, no, Ashley, we can't."

I shook my head. "No, you're right, we can't."

His nostrils flared, a muscle danced in his cheek and his arms tensed. "I want to give you pleasure too. Can you wait until tonight for me to make love to you?" His voice was tight and strained.

My pussy was buzzing, weeping for him. I glanced at the heavy door. It was shut tight. "No. That's too long to wait."

"So what do you think we should do?"

"You remember the scene in *Pounding Without Sound*?" I asked.

"When Marie and Travis are on the airplane, in the restroom?"

"Yes, and they have to be really quick and really quiet."

He nodded.

"So be really quick and really quiet."

He gulped, hesitated, then delved into the back pocket of his suit trousers and pulled out his wallet. "I've got a ribbed one."

My spine turned to dust and I clung to him for all I was worth. He was so bad, oh god, *we* were so bad. We were actually going to do this. "So what are you waiting for?" I managed.

He tore the wrapper open as I fumbled with his fly. My fingers would barely work, the glut of adrenaline in my system was so potent.

"Ashley," he said, stilling all movement. "Am I? Am I still the only one?"

Bashing my other fist on his shoulder, I frowned. "Of course, how can you even ask?"

He smirked. "Just checking. I love the fact that you've only known me, that I'm the only one to have touched and been inside your perfect little body."

"So quit talking and get inside me now." I pulled his erect cock from the gap in his trousers.

He grunted and pressed forward into my grip. "This is crazy."

"I know, we could both lose our jobs."

"So you retract your notice?"

"Oh yes."

Hastily he rolled on the condom. The ridges in the latex were big and wide. A tremble of anticipation besieged me as he bent his head and captured my mouth with his.

I slotted my fingers into the gusset of my panties and pulled them aside. His cock was there instantly, sliding forward. Suddenly all thoughts of the door opening and us being discovered left me. There was just Shane. He did this, it was a power he possessed. When I was with him he became my universe.

I tipped my pelvis and my butt cheeks lifted from the cool desk, getting the angle just right for his penetration. It took a couple of determined shunts before he was in. As soon as he was he rode up high and fast. The ridges were well defined and I could make them out smoothing over my internal flesh.

"Oh, yes, yes," I cried into his mouth.

"Shh," he murmured, "my secretary will hear."

I clamped my lips and clung to his shoulders. His suit jacket was thick and heavy beneath my fingers but the material, fine and smooth.

"Be quick," he said on a gasping breath. "Please, honey, be really quick."

"Yes, yes, I will."

His pubic bone was connecting lusciously with my clit. I curled my stockinged legs around his hips and locked my high heels together. The feel of his pants on my calves was wicked and naughty and reminded me that we weren't in bed. We were dressed and behaving hugely inappropriately. We were on a desk just like in *A Mistress for Midnight* when Georgina had corned Raif in the law chamber. She'd bent over the table with her dress thrown over her back, her butt bare as she tempted him to enter her. He hadn't been able to resist.

"Ah, fuck, I'm coming," Shane gasped into my ear. "Please, please come with me."

His desperate words tipped me over the edge and I claimed a hard, fast orgasm that had me panting his name and clinging to his body. Who would have known sex with the boss on his desk could be so damn satisfying?

We didn't linger. No sooner had Shane filled the condom than he was withdrawing and snapping it off.

I realigned my panties, stood and smoothed down my skirt. My breaths were rapid, my bra abrading my stiff nipples. My pussy was pulsing around nothing and my clit still bobbed within its hood.

"We really shouldn't have done that," he said breathlessly.

"I know." I wiped a film of sweat from my forehead and tried to flatten out my hair.

"What if someone had come in?"

"They didn't." I took the condom from him, wrapped it in my ratty handkerchief and shoved it deep in the waste paper bin. "It's okay. No one caught us."

His face suddenly creased into an almighty grin. "You," he said, "are such a bad influence on me. Like seriously, sex has never been so crazy, so imaginative or so damn risky until you came along."

Pouting, I jutted my hips. "What, little old me?"

"Yes, little old you, now quick, scarper. Go home, go back to your office. Whatever, but just be ready for me to collect you at 7:30. We're going to this thing at The Cow and Slipper together, as a couple. We may as well let everyone know what's what, because there is no way

I'm going to be sneaking around and pretending I'm not..." His voice trailed off.

"You're not what?"

He cleared his throat. "Not with you."

*****

We stood outside The Cow and Slipper, arms linked.

"You okay?" Shane asked, shoving his other hand into the deep pocket of his jacket. The north wind was bitter and howled down the street as if it was on a mission to rip the lampposts from their foundations.

"I'm fine," I said.

"I just want to check something."

"What?"

"Gareth."

"Gareth?"

"Yeah, he seemed pretty into you today. Is there anything I should know about?"

"Me and Gareth, no, nothing. He's okay but he's just a friend, a work friend."

"He seems very attentive of you."

"He's sweet, caring, always has been but he has no interest in getting in my knickers." I grinned.

Shane narrowed his eyes and bent his face to mine. "I'm sweet and caring too and I happen to like being in your knickers very much, you get what I'm saying?"

"Well, I've never thought of him like that, trust me, and if he thinks there's a chance of something happening between us then that's all it is, his thoughts."

Shane's lips touched mine, briefly. "Good, that's what I wanted to hear. Now come on, let's show the world we're a couple."

He pushed open the heavy door and stepped inside. The sound of merriment and the scent of beer engulfed me. Tugging my hand and forging through the crowd, Shane pulled me with him.

Big shoulders surrounded me and the guffaw of deep laughter filled the air. Ducking my head and allowing Shane to lead the way, I relished the moment of being looked after, protected. Any other time I would have had to shuffle my way through alone, apologizing and struggling to find my colleagues.

It took a few minutes to reach the quiet back corner Safe as Houses had claimed, but Shane had made it there quicker than I would have, even with me in tow.

"Shane," Derek said, slamming his pint on a table, standing and whacking his hand on Shane's shoulder. "So glad you made it, we were beginning to give up hope."

"Wouldn't have missed it," Shane said, grinning at the faces looking his way. "Anyone need a drink?"

I stood behind him and peered 'round his arm, spotted most of the sales staff, including Gareth, all the finance boys and Samantha the receptionist. I wished Dawn had been there, I could have done with her support at this moment in time—after I'd throttled her, that was.

"No, let me get you one," Gareth said, standing.

I felt Shane's body tense. It was well hidden, but I felt it in the hand holding mine and saw it in the twitch of his shoulders.

"It's great to have you on board, I wish you well," Gareth said. "What are you having, mate?"

My heart soared with relief. Gareth wasn't going to be a problem. And Gareth was the one who could have really rocked the boat.

"Ah, thanks, I'll have a Stella, but my round next." Shane turned to me. "What do you want, honey, a glass of white wine?"

He wasn't going to let me hide any longer. With a delicate twist of his wrist, he drew me in front of him.

I gulped and leaned my back into his chest. My knees felt weak, all eyes were on me.

All eyes were never on me!

"Ashley, poppet," Derek said, "you made it after all."

I nodded and tightened my grip on Shane's hand.

"She had a whopping headache," Shane said, returning the hand squeeze, "but it's been better since she had some medication, isn't that right?"

"Er, yes, it's much better now." I smiled in a self-conscious kind of way.

"So you're good for a glass of wine?" Gareth asked, glancing between me and Shane with a confused expression.

"Yes, yes, please."

"We're seeing each other," Shane said. He was looking at Gareth but the whole group were listening so he spoke loud enough to be heard by all. "Ashley is an amazing woman and I have very strong feelings for her. You may as well all know that now, because I'm the kind of guy that if something is going on, no matter what it is, I believe it should be out in the open."

"Here, here," Derek said, lifting his pint. "Here's to honesty and Shane and Ashley." He looked at me and winked.

Gareth stooped and pressed a light peck on my cheek. "I'm happy for you," he said. "You've been on your own too long."

I contained a sudden rush of fondness for him as Shane released my hand and wound his arm around my waist.

"White wine then, yes?" Gareth asked.

"Please."

"And a Stella," he directed at Shane.

"Yes, thanks."

Gareth stepped away and the hum of conversation resumed, Derek taking center stage with a golfing tale.

Shane tipped his head to my ear and I nestled into the perfect scoop of his body. "You remember the words you said in The Fenchurch?" he asked.

I turned my head and looked up at him. "You mean?"

"Yes, you know the ones I mean."

I nodded.

"Were they the truth, or rather, do you think they could be, one day?"

Nibbling my bottom lip, I nodded again. "Yes." I spun and looked into his eyes.

"Good, 'cause later I'll get you to say them again, and then, honey, I'm going to throw them right back at you."

Dipping his head, he touched his mouth to mine, soft and sweet and full of promise. I heard a cheer behind us as our workmates enjoyed our public display of affection, but it barely registered, all I could think of was telling Shane I loved him and having him say it too.

I sent a thanks across the miles to Dawn—love her, hate her, she'd kick-started my life and I would be eternally grateful for that despite the ups and downs along the way. But what path to love was without its mishaps? If it were, then there wouldn't be a story, and stories, sizzlingly naughty and hopelessly romantic stories, were one of my most favorite things in the world.

Chapter Nine

Six weeks later

The deserted Underground station was starkly lit and silent, the air smelled of fumes and grime.

"The last one will be here any minute," Shane said, hugging me close.

I stamped my cold feet on the ground and sank into him. He'd just treated me to a wonderful meal at a fancy Italian for Valentine's Day and my stomach was warm and full even if my extremities were chilled. He'd bought me a pretty pair of diamond earrings too, which I now wore, and we'd decided on Spain as a spring break to escape the never-ending UK winter.

All in all a perfect evening. We just had one more thing to do—the icing on the cake, the cherry on the top.

"It can't come soon enough," I said, pressing my cheek against the slightly scratchy wool of his jacket. "It's freezing."

"Ah, honey, you'll soon be basking in the sun, we'll have a look online tomorrow and get something booked."

A whoosh of air flowed from the black tunnel and the silver lines of track hummed.

Sudden shouts and the clacking of heels to my left caught my attention. I turned and saw two couples, hand in hand, spilling onto the platform giggling. Shane and I glanced at each other.

"It'll be okay," he said, his eyes sparkling. "Not exactly a busload of people."

I nodded and my heart picked up a notch as the train hurtled into the station. Fast and violent it raced past us, barely seeming to have its brakes on. I scanned the carriages as best I could, spotted a few passengers, but mainly it appeared empty.

Finally it drew to a stop and the doors hissed open.

"Come on, Georgina," Shane said with a devilish grin, "let's get on board."

The new arrivals on the platform picked a carriage near the front of the train as we dashed two more carriages down from where we'd seen the last passenger.

"Oh, Raif," I said, smirking as I glanced around our empty carriage. "It seems you have no one to protect you from me."

"As if I would need protecting from a woman," Shane said, dropping down on a purple padded seat and folding his arms.

I sidled up next to him, rolling my hips beneath my winter coat, my gaze heavy and a sexy smile on my lips. "We'll see about that."

The doors shut and the train suddenly lurched forward.

"Oh, shit," I yelped, staggering and flailing my arms.

"Careful." He grabbed me around the waist and tugged me down next to him.

I laughed and looked up into his face.

He lifted his eyebrows and pushed me back into a sitting position so I wasn't touching him. "I know all your sneaky little tricks, Georgina, they won't work with me."

"Mmm," I said, unbuttoning his coat and running my hands over his shirt. I smoothed my palm over his stomach and around his lean waist. "Maybe you shouldn't be so sure about that." I dipped my hand lower, over the hard leather of his belt to his groin. His erection was straining against his fly as I knew it would be. Shane had been looking forward to this scene from *A Mistress For Midnight* since I'd suggested it earlier when we'd swapped Valentine cards.

He sucked in a breath and a muscle in his cheek flexed.

"You want me," I said huskily, leaning up so my mouth was a whisper from his. "You want me here and now, just admit it."

"No, no that's not true."

"Then tell me, Raif, why have you been looking at me all day like you want to bend me over your office desk and fuck my brains out?"

His mouth twitched—that had been a line from the book but I think it was also pretty near the truth.

"That's a lie," he said, swallowing tightly.

The train was picking up speed now and we were jostling against each other. The black windows flashed every couple of seconds as lights in the tunnels whizzed by.

"It is true. I've felt your eyes burning onto my body all day. Seen you shifting on your seat during meetings, you know how I make you feel. You know how only *I* can make you come so hard you feel like your whole body is about to explode." I rubbed my hand up his hard cock, sought out the zipper and pulled it down.

"Last weekend was a mistake, Georgina, we never should have gone to The Ritz."

I glanced over my shoulder, checked we were still alone. "So does that mean you considered it a mistake when I did this to you in the shower?"

I pulled his cock through the gap in his boxers and the undone zip in his pants then dipped my head to his groin, all the time being careful not to expose him, just in case there were any secret cameras watching us.

"Ah, fuck," he said, helping me move his coat so I had better but still concealed access. "Seriously, Georgie, here?"

I couldn't answer. By now I was sinking low, taking his hot, hard shaft deep into my mouth. We didn't have long until the next station. Shane would have to be quick. I would have to use my entire repertoire of skills.

My hair fell forward around my ears as I plunged downward, creating a taut curve with my tongue to envelop his length.

"Ah, yes, fucking hell," he cursed above me, sliding his fingers through my hair.

I raised my head, slid my lips up his shaft and felt his slit skim over my palate. I could taste the salty hint of pre-cum and hoped to hell more was on the way—fast.

I bobbed up as the train twisted around a corner. I sank back down, creating a strong suction. I'd enjoyed lots of exquisite flavors tonight but this was my favorite by far. Shane's desire and pleasure was the ultimate taste experience for me.

"Georgie, this is so bad but so good, god damn you, woman, I'm coming."

His cock went rigid and thick. My heart pounded—the sound of the train mixing with the short, sharp gasps Shane emitted was highly erotic. Suddenly he was there, spurting, coming in my mouth. I gulped and swallowed him, lapping up the copious liquid and slurping on his erection.

"Fuck, yes," he hissed, jerking his hips up and bashing the head of his cock into the back of my throat.

I groaned too, the bliss of giving him a fast, illicit orgasm was a total turn-on.

As soon as the last spurt oozed out I lifted my head and quickly tucked him back into his pants. He was still gasping for air when I straightened and looked at his face.

"You are an evil woman," he said, his eyes flashing and a couple of beads of sweat sitting on his top lip.

"Evil but irresistible."

He touched his lips to mine and wrapped me in his arms. "Totally irresistible, and tonight, when we get back to my place, I'm going to show you exactly how much I want you every damn minute of every damn day, even though I know I shouldn't."

"Mmm, I can't wait." I traced the outline of his stubble from his ear to the curve of his cheek. I knew full well he'd more than live up to his words.

He tipped his head and sighed. "Ashley, I mean it."

"What?"

"This is me speaking now, not Raif, I want you every minute of every day, I never thought I'd feel like this. It's so much more than anything else I've ever had."

"Me too."

He was silent.

I sensed there was more. "Shane?"

"Move your stuff over to mine, fill up some of those empty drawers and cupboards. I can't bear it when you go to your place and I'm on my own. We belong together even if it's just watching TV or cooking dinner."

A knot of excitement grew in my chest. That was exactly how I felt. Whenever we were apart I was clock watching until we were together again.

"Are you sure?"

"Of course I'm sure. Jesus, I start missing you half an hour before you even say goodbye." He cupped my cheeks in his palms. "I love you so much, Ashley, I might not be ready for marriage again but I want you there when I go to bed and there when I wake up, every night, every morning, without exception."

I lifted up from the seat and threw my arms around his neck. "Since you asked so nicely then yes, yes I will move some stuff over."

"And we'll see how it goes."

"Yes, I'll see how it goes living with my boss."

He laughed. "Somehow I think you have your boss exactly where you want him."

"Mmm, not right this minute, but give me another half an hour and I have a feeling that will be the case."

He grinned then kissed me deep and lovingly. Emotions and feelings, promises and hope poured into my heart. We worked hard and played hard and I looked forward to everything the future held for us. Because if we were together then life was as hot and sunny as the most beautiful summer's day even if it was cold and frosty outside.

THE END

About the Author

Based in the UK Lily Harlem is an award-winning, USA Today best-selling author of sexy romance. She's a complete floozy when it comes to genres and pairings writing from heterosexual kink, to gay paranormal and everything in-between. She's also very partial to a happily ever after.

One thing you can be sure of, whatever book you pick up by Ms Harlem, is it will be wildly romantic and deliciously sexy. Enjoy!

Website *lilyharlem.com*

Printed in Great Britain
by Amazon

54911773R00090